Her proximity to the cowboy scrambled her thoughts, weakened her resolve.

Like now. She should be knocking his hand from her shoulder. Shrugging him off. Assuring him she could handle anything.

Instead she tilted her head, brushing the back of his hand with her hair, allowing the warmth of his touch to spread through her body like a salve to her frayed nerves.

She breathed out a soft sigh. "Maybe I don't have a choice, Rafe. Maybe something's headed my way whether I like it or not. And this time I can't stop it, can't run away."

He wedged a finger beneath her chin, tilting her head back. The gaze from his blue eyes burned into hers. "Whatever comes at you, Dana, I'll be right beside you to take it on."

He brushed the whisper of a kiss across her lips before slamming the car door.

Placing a fingertip on her burning lips, Dana wondered if Rafe realized he posed as great a threat to her as this serial killer.

CAROL ERICSON

THE SHERIFF OF SILVERHILL

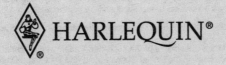

HARLEQUIN®

TORONTO • NEW YORK • LONDON
AMSTERDAM • PARIS • SYDNEY • HAMBURG
STOCKHOLM • ATHENS • TOKYO • MILAN • MADRID
PRAGUE • WARSAW • BUDAPEST • AUCKLAND

To the wonderful ladies of GIAM.
Thanks for your motivation.

Recycling programs
for this product may
not exist in your area.

ISBN-13: 978-0-373-69451-8

THE SHERIFF OF SILVERHILL

ABOUT THE AUTHOR

Carol Ericson lives with her husband and two sons in Southern California, home of state-of-the-art cosmetic surgery, wild freeway chases, palm trees bending in the Santa Ana winds and a million amazing stories. These stories, along with hordes of virile men and feisty women, clamor for release from Carol's head. It makes for some interesting headaches until she sets them free to fulfill their destinies and her readers' fantasies. To find out more about Carol, her books and her strange headaches, please visit her Web site at www.carolericson.com, "where romance flirts with danger."

Books by Carol Ericson

HARLEQUIN INTRIGUE
1034—THE STRANGER AND I
1079—A DOCTOR-NURSE-ENCOUNTER
1117—CIRCUMSTANTIAL MEMORIES
1184—THE SHERIFF OF SILVERHILL

CAST OF CHARACTERS

Dana Croft—An FBI agent with the Indian Country Crimes Unit, she returns to the Ute reservation outside of Silverhill, Colorado, where she grew up, to investigate a serial killer. But the investigation becomes complicated by the powers of clairvoyance she rejected years ago... and the man she left behind.

Rafe McClintock—The sheriff of Silverhill must join forces with the FBI, including his high school sweetheart, to solve a series of murders. Can his love for the woman who walked out on him save her from her own dangerous secrets?

Lenny Driscoll—Dana's stepfather exploited her mother's powers, which led to her death. Dana wants to make sure she doesn't meet the same fate at his hands.

Joshua Trujillo—An old friend of Dana's, but his jokes about her dumping him start getting a little too serious, perhaps serious enough to send him over the edge of reason.

Ben Whitecotton—He's intent on preserving the Southern Ute culture and seems to have disdain for those Native Americans who don't embrace their heritage as he thinks they should.

Alicia Clifton—The one victim of the Headband Killer who doesn't seem to fit the profile...until her secret is revealed.

Auntie Mary—Dana's great-aunt and a Southern Ute shaman, she sees danger in Dana's future but is powerless to stop it.

Kelsey Croft—Dana's daughter doesn't know her father, Rafe McClintock, and Rafe doesn't know her. Will Kelsey's gift of clairvoyance destroy her before Rafe can claim her as his own?

Chapter One

FBI Agent Dana Croft ducked beneath the yellow crime scene tape snapping in the dry wind that whipped across the construction site. She joined her partner, Agent Steve Lubeck, squatting beside the body of a young woman—the third in two months.

Dana had been planning a visit to the Southern Ute Reservation where she grew up…just hadn't planned on spending it tracking a serial killer.

Slipping on a pair of latex gloves, Dana crouched next to the woman's head, her dark hair matted with blood and sticking to her cheek. Blood also stained the bandana wrapped around her forehead.

"Do you know her?" Steve slid one gloved finger beneath the victim's hair, lifting it from her face.

Dana scanned the woman's features—a pretty girl with too much makeup and staring, lifeless eyes. She didn't recognize her, but everyone else on the reservation would know her and her business. The small-town atmosphere of a reservation usually made solving crimes for the Indian Country Crimes unit easy.

But this wasn't racketeering or casino theft; this was murder.

"Nope." Dana shook her head. "But then it's been several

years since I've been back. I probably know her parents or grandparents, though."

Dana squeezed her eyes shut and gulped in a few breaths of crisp autumn air. The young woman splayed out on the hard earth with her long black hair and mocha skin reminded Dana of her own daughter, Kelsey. Could she handle this assignment? She'd been with the FBI for almost six years and with the Indian Country Crimes unit for four of those years, but she'd never investigated a serial killer on a reservation. This hit hard. This hit home.

"The construction crew discovered the body when they got here this morning. They called the sheriff of the Ute Reservation, Emmett Starr. You know him?"

"Yeah, I know Emmett. Where is he?"

"He was tied up with something else, but he called me right away and sent his guys." Steve waved his arm toward the two cops combing the area for a footprint, blood, a piece of clothing, any small piece of evidence. "Emmett should be here soon."

"I think that's him now." Shading her eyes and squinting at the squad car churning up dust on the road, Dana pushed to her feet.

The car pulled up parallel to the crime scene, and Emmett shot out of the driver's side. "Damn. I can't believe we have another one. I guess it's official now—we have a serial killer on our hands."

He strode toward Dana and swept her up in a hug. "Good to see you, Dana."

"You don't seem surprised that I'm here."

Emmett jerked his thumb toward Steve. "Agent Lubeck told me you were coming on the scene to help out. That's good you're working in the Indian Country Crimes unit."

The passenger door of Emmett's squad car swung open, and Dana swiveled her head around. One long, lean, denim-clad leg appeared. The long, lean body followed.

Dana's breath hitched in her throat and her heart skittered in her chest as the rangy cowboy in the white hat sauntered toward her, sliding his cell phone into his shirt pocket. He tipped his hat back from his face and grinned. "Hey, Dana."

Dana swallowed, her throat tight, as she looked up into the perpetually amused blue eyes of Rafe McClintock.

The man who still had a hold on her heart.

The man who haunted her dreams.

The father of her child.

"What are you doing here?" Dana folded her arms, trapping her trembling hands next to her body. Rafe didn't seem surprised to see her, either. Everyone on the reservation must know she'd returned to assist in this investigation.

Emmett moved to the side. "I'm sorry. You two know each other, don't you? Rafe and I were in Silverhill, discussing the second murder when I got Agent Lubeck's call. Agent Lubeck, this is Sheriff Rafe McClintock. The second murder occurred in his jurisdiction."

As Steve and Rafe shook hands, Dana zeroed in on the badge pinned to Rafe's chest. Why hadn't Auntie Mary told her Rafe was back in Silverhill? She might have had some time to prepare, to steel herself against this rush of emotion cascading through her body.

"Y-you're a San Juan County Sheriff?"

"Yeah, I moved back to Colorado about six months ago and went through the academy. Silverhill elected me sheriff when Sheriff Ballard retired after his son's murder."

"I heard about Zack Ballard's murder." She pursed her lips as she shook her head. "I'm glad Sheriff Ballard retired, but the good people of Silverhill sure embraced an inexperienced sheriff for the top job quickly. But then you *are* a McClintock."

There. Better put Rafe in his place right here and now.

He raised his brows, laughter lighting his eyes. God, he saw right through her. She'd fooled him once but he was no longer the tall, skinny, sandy-haired boy she'd first spotted in the hallway of Silverhill High.

She *would* have to feel an insane attraction to the richest and most popular boy in the school. She lived the cliché of every teen movie, featuring the all-American boy and the girl from the wrong side of the tepee. Only their teen movie didn't end with happily-ever-after.

"I'm not inexperienced. I know Silverhill like the back of my hand, and I worked as a cop in L.A. for almost four years before moving back here. Of course, you wouldn't know that since you disappeared right after high school. Georgetown, right?"

"Yeah, Georgetown."

Emmett cleared his throat. "I hate to break up this…er… happy reunion, but what do you have on this latest murder? Is it like the other two?"

Steve and Dana led Rafe and Emmett to the body and Emmett crouched down. "Dear God. This is Louella's girl, Holly."

"Louella Sams?" Dana clapped a hand over her mouth. Louella was about fifteen years ahead of her in school, but Dana knew the family. The personal aspect hit her hard but if she let it affect her, the Bureau would yank her off the investigation. And she wanted in on this investigation.

"Louella Thompson now. She let Holly run a little wild, but nobody deserves this kind of ending." Emmett clutched his hat to his chest and mumbled a few words over Holly's still form.

Dana recognized the Southern Ute chant for the soul of the

dead to speed its passage to the heavens. She bit her lip. It had been so long, she'd almost forgotten the words of the chant.

Steve cleared his throat. "The M.O. is the same as the other two murders. The blood on Holly's face is from a split lip. Looks like the killer backhanded her, but he strangled her like the other two and dumped her at a construction site."

"And he left his signature." Rafe pointed to the bandana wrapped around Holly's forehead with the feather stuck in the back.

Dana clenched her jaw. That's the detail law enforcement was hiding from the media. The killer had placed the crude Indian headband around each of the victims after he murdered them. So far, all of the murdered women were full or half Native American—like her. Was this maniac on some kind of one-man ethnic cleansing spree? Apparently, his wrath didn't extend to males or anyone over the age of thirty. All of the victims were young, female and pretty.

Rafe gestured to the ground. "Tire tracks?"

Steve shrugged. "This area is crisscrossed with tire tracks. Nothing stands out, and so far Emmett's officers haven't found a damn thing…just like the other two murders."

Scuffing the toe of his boot into the sand, Rafe said, "Obviously, the construction site is just a dumping ground. He does the deed elsewhere."

Dana appraised Rafe from beneath lowered lashes. His handsome face creased into real concern, and Dana realized she faced a man, not the carefree boy she'd loved enough to leave ten years ago.

That knowledge scared the hell out of her.

The four of them discussed the details of the murders, two now on the Southern Ute Reservation, until the ambulance arrived. Any more evidence they hoped to find would have to come from the victim's body. If the killer hit her before he strangled her, maybe Holly put up a fight for her life and scratched her murderer or pulled out his hair.

They agreed to meet later that evening at Rafe's office at the sheriff's station in Silverhill to compare notes after following their different leads. Rafe jogged to the ambulance before the EMTs loaded the stretcher bearing Holly's body.

Dana's heart picked up speed as Rafe bent his head in conversation, a lock of sun-streaked hair falling over one eye. She'd have to put aside her personal feelings to get through this investigation. Since one of the bodies had turned up outside the boundaries of the reservation, Rafe had jurisdiction over that case and she'd have to work with him.

But not for long.

The FBI would move in and take over. Just like they always did.

But until then, she'd shove memories of Rafe and their high school romance aside. And their daughter? Could she shove her aside as well?

"What do you think, Dana?"

She spun around. Emmett stood behind her, his hands buried in his pockets as he watched the EMTs collapse the stretcher to slide it into the van.

Lifting a shoulder, she said, "Looks like our guy has struck again, but Silverhill is a small town and everyone knows everyone else's business on the reservation. We'll find him."

"Can you help? Did you touch Holly with your bare hands?"

Dana sucked in a sharp breath and froze. Emmett wasn't referring to the help Dana could offer as an FBI agent. He wanted her to use the "gift."

Closing her eyes, she ran a hand through her hair and clasped the nape of her neck.

"You are gifted." Emmett's voice floated between them, almost a whisper.

"Don't call me that."

"Sorry." He held up his hands. "But everyone knows the powers of clairvoyance travel through the women in our particular Southern Ute tribe. Auntie Mary is gifted and her sister Fanny, your grandmother, had the gift, and your mother, Ronnie."

"A lot of good it did my mother." Once Dana's worthless stepfather had found out about Mom's sensitivity, he had exploited it, forcing her to work during the summer months selling cheap jewelry, telling fortunes and casting spells of love and protection when Mom couldn't even find those for herself.

Dana ran her hands across her face as if clearing cobwebs. "Besides, I'm only half Ute, so the gift obviously skipped me. See you at the meeting, Emmett."

As Dana swept past him, Emmett muttered behind her, "Or you choose not to embrace it."

Dana stalked to her rental car, hands fisted. Her second day back on the reservation and already her past was crowding in on her.

"Dana."

She glanced up as Rafe waved and strode toward her, his boots crunching the gravel beneath his feet. Her past was crowding in, all right, from all directions.

"Can I pick you up for the meeting tonight? I haven't seen your aunt Mary in a while. You are staying with her, aren't you?"

She clicked her remote and settled her back against the car. "I don't need a ride. This is a murder investigation, not the high school prom."

"I know. You dumped me before the prom."

"You remember that?" *Big mistake.* She did not want to

traipse down memory lane with Rafe. That path would surely lead to one nine-year old, brown-eyed secret named Kelsey.

Hooking his thumb in his belt loop, he grinned. "Like it was yesterday. You were the only girl who ever shot me down."

"Oh, I don't know. I remember succumbing to the famous McClintock charm pretty quickly."

"Yeah, you had your way with me and *then* shot me down."

Dana almost doubled over from the sharp pain that stabbed her gut. If they didn't catch this killer fast, allowing her to escape Silverhill and the reservation, she'd fall under this man's spell again. And once he found out she'd kept Kelsey from him all these years, he'd shoot *her* down.

"Let's not go there." She made a cross with her fingers, holding it up between them. "We have a killer to catch."

"I don't have a problem mixing business with pleasure."

Dana's gaze tripped over Rafe's sensuous mouth and got hooked on his deep blue eyes. "I'll bet you don't."

But if Rafe ever discovered they had a daughter together, there'd be nothing pleasurable about his response.

Nothing pleasurable at all.

DANA DROPPED into the overstuffed, floral chair and stretched out her legs, resting her feet on top of the high heels she'd kicked off before washing the dinner dishes.

Auntie Mary plucked the reading glasses from her nose and folded her hands over the book in her lap. "You could've left those for me. I didn't invite you to stay here to do my chores."

Dana wiggled her toes. "I know that, but you do have an ulterior motive."

"I don't need an ulterior motive to invite my niece, who's working in the area anyway, to stay with me." Auntie Mary widened her eyes in mock indignation.

"Rosemary chicken, mashed potatoes and gravy, fresh string beans from your garden and homemade apple pie to finish me off. You went to a lot of trouble, but it's not going to work."

"Is Holly Thompson another victim of this serial killer?"

"We think so, but I can't discuss the case with you."

"Interesting that the killer keeps dumping bodies of young Ute women at construction sites. Maybe he's trying to make a point." She shrugged and ran a gnarled hand through her cropped, gray hair. "The old ways are changing too fast, and all this money pouring in from the oil down south only hastens the demise of our culture. Dances, songs and worship have been replaced by reality TV and Xboxes."

"Unemployment and poverty have been replaced by jobs and a good standard of living."

"Do you have to throw out the baby with the bathwater?" Auntie Mary cupped her hands in a scooping motion.

"Nobody's trying to do that. I see that Ben Whitecotton is completing the project of a Southern Ute cultural center."

Auntie Mary leveled a finger at her, and Dana could almost feel a shaft of heat scorching her from across the room. "You approve of all the changes."

"I'm proud of my Southern Ute heritage." Dana crossed her arms, bunching her fists. "I just don't believe in all the mumbo jumbo stuff."

"You have the sacred gift." Auntie Mary dropped her arm and closed her eyes. "And you choose to dismiss it."

"What about my mother?" Dana jumped from the chair and took a turn around the small room. "She did worse than dismiss it. She tarnished it, used it for monetary gain."

"That was her husband's idea."

At the mention of her stepfather, Dana ground her teeth. She'd detested her stepfather, Lenny Driscoll, ever since she was five years old when he oozed his way into her mother's life. "If I never see Lenny again, it will be too soon for me."

Auntie Mary gripped the cane resting against the arm of her chair and pushed to her feet. "I may as well tell you since you'll be here for a while. Lenny's been hanging around the reservation."

Dana choked, her throat suddenly dry and constricted. "Lenny's here? What does he want? No, don't answer that. He wants a piece of the oil proceeds."

"That about sums it up."

"Mom died before the oil was discovered. Even if she hadn't, I don't think Lenny is entitled to any of the profit. He doesn't have one drop of Southern Ute blood."

Except on his hands.

"He's working all the angles." Auntie Mary glanced at the old-fashioned clock on the kitchen wall. "Isn't it time for your meeting with Rafe McClintock? You didn't mention you'd seen him this morning."

Dana jerked her head up and met her aunt's steady gaze from luminous dark eyes. Auntie Mary always could read her mind, and Dana didn't believe it had anything to do with that gift thing.

She pulled the keys out of her purse and swung them around her index finger. "Yeah, I saw him. You didn't tell me he was Sheriff McClintock of Silverhill."

"When are you going to tell him about Kelsey?"

"Who said I was?"

"He deserves to know, Dana. He's a good man."

"He didn't come after me." Dana clutched her purse to her chest with clammy hands. She'd already come to the same conclusion as Auntie Mary, but the thought of telling Rafe about his nine-year-old daughter scared the hell out of her. Rafe hated secrets and lies.

"He was a boy and starting college himself." She tapped her cane on the floor. "Besides you hurt him deeply. His mother abandoned him and his two brothers when she left Ralph McClintock. When you took off without a backward glance or explanation, he must've felt that abandonment all over again."

Tilting her head back, Dana laughed. "Please. As I recall, he recovered pretty quickly with Melanie. Or was it Belinda or Shari? He could have his pick, and I'm sure Pam approved of those girls."

"Don't let his stepmother scare you off this time. You've turned out nothing like your mother. To draw comparisons between the two of you is ridiculous."

Dana crossed the room and planted a kiss on her aunt's weathered cheek. "Let me worry about Rafe. Thanks for dinner. I'll probably be home late. Don't wait up."

Auntie Mary straightened her spine and narrowed her eyes. "Be careful out there. There's a killer on the loose, and you're in danger."

A chill rippled along Dana's flesh and she gripped her purse tighter. Unlike Dana, Auntie Mary did use her gift and she was right more often than Dana cared to admit. Pure coincidence.

"There's always an element of danger when you're investigating a series of murders. It comes with the job."

Shaking her head, Auntie Mary collapsed in her chair. "But this is different, isn't it? This killer is targeting young Native American women…and you're half Ute."

"Don't worry." Hitching her purse over her shoulder, Dana waved. "See you later."

Dana locked the dead bolt behind her. As she approached her car, a low growl rumbled from the underbrush at the edge of the driveway. She spun around, gripping her car keys in one clenched fist. Squinting into the darkness, her gaze tumbled across bushes and scrub, the glow from the lamppost touching their leaves with a blurry light. Auntie Mary's house sat on the edge of the reservation and blackness smothered the rest of the landscape where ominous shapes hunched and waited.

Would wild animals from the mountains venture this close to a populous area? Her gaze swept from side to side, taking in the unrelenting wilderness hugging the clearing of reservation homes. The reservation didn't exactly occupy the hub of civilization.

She grasped the door handle of her rental car and tugged. A louder, more menacing growl sent a river of chills up her spine as she yanked open the car door. Her keys slid from her clammy hand, and she swore as she crouched to retrieve them.

A rush of damp air surrounded her. Cold fingers gripped the back of her neck, pushing her to the ground, immobilizing her. She froze in place, her knees grinding into the rough gravel. Her jaw locked, and she squeezed her eyes shut.

A whisper as soft as the wind brushed her ear. "Go away. You might be next."

Chapter Two

The hand grasping Dana's neck melted away, and she hunched her shoulders against the cold vice that lingered even as her attacker relinquished his grip. The bushes rustled, and she rolled her head to the side, picking out two golden orbs glowing in the night as if suspended in the darkness.

Feral eyes.

As the eyes faded in the darkness, Dana seemed to recover from a trance. Her rigid muscles relaxed and she slumped forward, leaning her forehead against the car door.

A footstep crunched the gravel next to her and a scream ripped from her throat.

"Dana, what the hell happened? What are you doing on the ground?"

Blinking, Dana tried to focus her gaze on a pair of cowboy boots. Safety. Security. Rafe.

"S-someone attacked me." She rubbed her eyes and grabbed the handle of the car door to struggle to her feet.

Rafe cursed and hooked his arms beneath hers, pulling her up and into his embrace. She sank against his broad chest, inhaling his clean, masculine scent, which seemed to revive her senses.

"Where'd he go?"

She raised her arm and with a shaky finger, pointed toward the underbrush. Rafe withdrew his weapon and gripped her shoulder. "You're going back inside."

"Dana? What's going on?" An oblong of light appeared where Auntie Mary opened her front door.

"Go." Rafe gave her a shove from behind and stalked toward the bushes.

"No!" Dana lunged toward him, grabbing his forearm. "Don't go in there, Rafe."

He cupped her face with one hand. "Don't worry. Get inside the house."

Dana stumbled toward Auntie Mary, who encircled her waist with one sinewy arm and drew her onto the porch. A beam of light from Rafe's flashlight pierced the darkness as he crashed through the underbrush.

Dana held her breath, watching the foliage engulf him. Would Rafe's gun be any match for what awaited him in the darkness?

Auntie Mary patted her arm. "He's going to be fine. What happened?"

"A man attacked me from behind while I was getting into my car."

Auntie Mary gasped and squeezed Dana's hand. "He's come after you sooner than I expected."

"He didn't come after me, at least not with murder on his mind. He whispered a warning. He may not even be the killer. Maybe it's some sicko playing a joke. A serial murder investigation brings all the wackos out of the closet."

With each sensible phrase she uttered, Dana gained a foothold back to reality.

"Did you get a look at him?"

"No. He came at me from behind, grabbed my neck."

"You didn't twist around to see him or go for your weapon?" Auntie Mary's dark eyes seemed to bore into her very soul, and Dana turned away to stare at the bushes where Rafe disappeared.

She didn't want to tell Auntie Mary about the growling or the yellow eyes or her trancelike state. She shook her head to dispel the images from her youth at Auntie Mary's knee, listening to the tales of the Ute spirits who took the forms of animals—birds, rabbits, bears and the most powerful of all…the wolf. The hand that grabbed the back of her neck and the voice that uttered the warning belonged to a man…a dangerous one. She may have imagined the rest in her terror.

"My gun was in my purse. I figured if I went for it, he'd kill me."

Rafe crashed back through the underbrush, saving her from another assault of Auntie Mary's questions.

He holstered his weapon and brushed bits of leaves and twigs from his shirt. He walked to the porch and balanced one foot on the first step. "Nothing. What happened out here, Dana?"

She recounted her story about dropping her keys and being grabbed from behind, leaving out the wolf bits. She didn't need Rafe questioning her sanity. "And then he warned me to go away, that I might be next."

"It's the killer." He scooped her back into his arms, and it felt so right. But she was an FBI agent here to do a job, not a love-struck teenager.

"Maybe not." She disentangled herself from his warmth, his protective embrace. "He might be some nut who knows I'm investigating the murders."

"Either way, you need protection. Why didn't you use your weapon?"

Dana didn't want to tell Rafe about her trancelike feeling. "My gun's in my purse. I didn't want to risk going for it."

Rafe rolled his eyes. "What are they teaching you out there at Langley?"

Dana folded her arms across her chest. "What are you doing here, anyway? I told you I didn't need a ride into town."

"I had business on the reservation. I figured I'd pick you up on the way. Emmett's already in Silverhill. It's a good thing I came out here."

Dana turned to Auntie Mary. "Are you going to be safe here tonight? Maybe you should stay with Alice and Gerald next door until I get home."

"Nonsense." Auntie Mary's hands fluttered. "I'm neither young nor pretty. I don't have anything to worry about. Besides, the aura of danger I see encompasses you, not me."

"Aura of danger?" Rafe jerked his head up.

Dana shot Auntie Mary a look through narrowed eyes and snorted. "Vague superstitions. That's all. Just vague superstitions."

As Rafe placed his hand on her back to guide her toward the car, Dana stared into the blackness and saw…nothing.

Nothing at all.

DANA HAD A SECRET.

Rafe clicked his seat belt into place, started the engine and glanced to his right. Damn, despite her recent scare, the woman looked good enough to lick up one side and down the other.

Her appearance at the murder scene this morning hadn't surprised him. Emmett told him she was coming out to assist the other agent, Steve Lubeck, in the investigation of the murders of two Southern Ute women—and then the murderer struck again on the day after her arrival. Coincidence?

After the attack on Dana tonight, the protective instinct that landed him in trouble with her ten years ago surged through his veins once again. She didn't like being coddled. Maybe that's why she broke it off with him…he'd smothered her with too much attention. Strong women didn't like smothering. That's why his mom left.

Her aunt Mary obviously hadn't told her about his return to Silverhill, but then why should she? He and Dana had a high school romance that didn't last. Nothing earth-shattering about that.

At least that's what he'd been trying to tell himself these past ten years.

Dana sighed and tucked her dark, stylishly cut hair behind her ear. The hairstyle, longer in the front and bobbed in the back, gave her a polished, sophisticated look, as did her silk wool pantsuit and sky-high heels.

But Rafe remembered the leggy girl with the cutoff shorts, bare feet and the long, almost black hair that hung right down to her behind. He recalled how she trailed her hair down his naked body as they made love in the caves above Silverhill, the secrecy of their desire heightening their passion.

He sucked in a breath, jerking the steering wheel of the car.

"You okay?" Dana drew her straight, dark brows over her nose.

"What really happened outside your aunt's house?" Rafe relaxed his grip on the wheel and shifted forward in his seat. "From what I know of you and from what I've heard, you don't back down from a fight so easily."

"Easily? The guy came at me from behind and clamped his hand around the back of my neck. I didn't know if he had a gun or a knife on him, and I didn't want to find out the hard way."

"Sorry." He brushed her arm. "You're right. You played it safe."

Too safe. Without visible evidence of a weapon, most

trained law enforcement officers would've tried to take the guy down. Something didn't click. He tightened his jaw. Growing up in a household full of lies and secrets taught him to hate deception.

She snorted. "I guess it's not how a McClintock would've handled it, huh?"

Rafe raised his brows. She made *McClintock* sound like a dirty word. When had she developed such a dislike for his family?

After their relationship during their high school years, she dumped him, even before graduation. Pam, his stepmom, told him Dana probably just dated him for his family's money and connections and dumped him when she got that full scholarship to Georgetown, but that didn't make sense. Dana was the smartest girl in school. There was no question she'd get a full ride somewhere. She didn't need his family's money or connections.

"I'm not second-guessing you, Dana. We all do what we have to do out there to survive. Just be careful. Maybe you shouldn't stay on the reservation with your aunt Mary."

Without turning around, Dana said, "Who appointed you my guardian? Auntie Mary worries enough."

"I remember."

She swung around and tilted her head. "Do you?"

"Like it was yesterday." He continued recklessly, "The blanket I spread out in the cave. The flower petals you showered all over to mask the dank smell. Your sexy, smooth skin under my fingertips."

"Stop right there." Dana held up her hands and he captured one in his own.

"Why did you run, Dana? What were you afraid of?" He gripped her hand, running his thumb along her knuckles.

Dana turned her head toward the window and blew out her breath, creating a patch of condensation on the glass. "Your stepmother didn't approve of our relationship."

Rafe shrugged. "Yeah, Pam kind of had it in for you. Never stopped me though."

Dana drew an *X* through the moisture on the glass. "Rafe, your stepmother is a bigot. She didn't like me because I was half Ute Indian."

"Pam's not my favorite person, either, but nothing she ever said made a damn bit of difference to me. Is that why you left, because my stepmother was a bigot?"

She snatched her hand away and pointed out the window. "Look. Emmett and Steve are already here."

Rafe clenched his teeth. Looked like Dana didn't have any interest in replaying their failed romance, or was it just a high school crush?

As soon as he swung his car into the reserved parking space in front of the station and pulled to a stop, Dana pushed open the door and launched out of the car. Whatever she'd feared from him ten years ago, it still existed.

By the time Rafe got out of the car, Dana had already apprised Emmett and Steve of the evening's activities. Rafe stood at the edge of their circle, listening as Dana finished her story. They didn't seem to find anything amiss in the fact that she hadn't tried to nail her attacker. The FBI always did things a little differently from local law enforcement anyway.

Emmett scratched his chin. "Did you see anything out there after the attack, Rafe?"

"A few freshly broken twigs and trampled underbrush, but the road into the reservation doesn't pass that way. Dana's assailant either took off on foot into the hills or he doubled back into the reservation."

Steve swore. "Cocky SOB, isn't he? FBI agent comes to town and the next day he's warning her."

"Wait a minute." Dana wedged her hands on her hips. "What makes you all so sure this is our serial killer? We all know the nuts and wannabes come out of the woodwork during an investigation like this. Maybe this guy just wants to get close to the action."

"Maybe, maybe not. But you need to be more aggressive in the use of your weapon, Agent Croft." Rafe patted his own gun, holstered over his shoulder. "If you'd gone for your gun, we might be interviewing a suspect right now...or bagging a dead body."

Rolling her eyes, Dana pushed past him. "Well, we're not doing either, Sheriff McClintock. So why don't we go inside this little hovel you call a sheriff's station and get to work."

Okay, maybe he deserved that after his own cheap shot, but she'd bruised his ego on the ride over here. Rafe shrugged his shoulders at the other men, their mouths hanging open, and followed Dana across the sidewalk to his...hovel.

Once inside, Rafe tossed his hat onto his desk and introduced the others to Brice Kellog, who was manning the station and the phones. The other sheriff's deputy on duty had patrol. Silverhill couldn't afford to put more than one officer on patrol at a time and Shelly, their dispatcher and receptionist, worked the day shift.

Like it or not, that's why they needed the FBI for an investigation like this, but Rafe planned to solve the case before the fibbies called in their big guns. He didn't want them to upstage him in his own town where he accepted full responsibility for the residents' safety.

Rafe gestured toward a round table next to the single interview room. "We can work over there."

Brice shot up from his chair. "Can I sit in on the meeting, Sheriff?"

"You can listen in, but I need you manning the phones and finishing that paperwork."

A flash of anger distorted Brice's features for a moment before he dropped his gaze. "Okay."

Rafe knew the young sheriff's deputy wanted in on the murder investigation, but he couldn't afford to spare him from the other duties. "I'll fill you in later."

They all dragged their files out of their briefcases and bags and dropped them onto the table.

Emmett started since some local boys found the first body in his jurisdiction—on the reservation. "Lindy Spode grew up here, went to Silverhill High School and worked as a waitress at the Miner's Café. She liked to party, and she frequented clubs in Durango. Two days before her murder, she'd been club hopping there."

"Holly Thompson, the victim today, also hung out at clubs in Durango." Steve hunched forward. "Did you show Lindy's picture around in Durango?"

"One bartender remembered her, but she was with girl-friends. Came with them, left with them."

"But this club scene could be a connection." Dana shuffled through some papers.

"I hate to be the spoiler here, but Alicia Clifton, the second victim, was no club hopper." Rafe tapped his finger on the desk. "She was in college, had a part-time job and helped out at the reservation school."

"Great, two party girls and Mother Teresa." Steve slumped back in his chair.

They continued to discuss the women's friends, hangouts and ex-boyfriends, and made a plan to share all their information going forward. The FBI's restraint surprised Rafe. Usually they moved in and took over, but Steve seemed willing to listen to what he and Emmett had to say about the cases. Maybe Steve was relying on Dana to lead the way, since this was Southern Ute territory, but Steve had been with the Indian Country Crimes unit for over fifteen years. He knew his way around a reservation.

If they all continued to cooperate, they'd nail this guy without further interference from the FBI.

"What about the calling card?" Dana bit her lip, her eyes darting around the table. "What's the significance of the crude Indian headband?"

Emmett splayed his hands on the tabletop and blew out a long breath. "So far he's been targeting Southern Ute women. Could be one of our own, could be some white guy on a mission."

Dana hunched her shoulders. "I hope not. Do you hear any rumblings on the reservation, Emmett?"

"There's a lot of fear, a little anger and some speculation since you came to town, Dana."

Dana shoved back from the table, almost knocking her chair to the floor. "Is there a bathroom around here, Sheriff?"

"Around the corner." Rafe pointed to the hallway on the other side of his desk.

As Dana turned the corner, Rafe swiveled his head back toward Emmett. "What speculation are you talking about?"

Emmett rubbed his hands on the thighs of his jeans and shot a glance toward the bathroom. "You know Dana's gifted?"

"Sure. She was the smartest girl in school, valedictorian even." Rafe scratched his chin. Did the entire reservation think Dana was going to catch this killer because she was valedictorian?

"I don't mean gifted that way. The Southern Ute, like most

Native American tribes, have shamans. They can see the future, cast spells and communicate with the spirit world. In our tradition, we call this having the gift and those who have it, gifted. Only women are gifted in our tribe, and it's passed down through families. The females in Dana's family are all gifted, but Dana chose to reject that part of her heritage."

Rafe's brows shot up. Maybe that's why Dana left him. She saw a vision of their future together and it stunk. "She never told me any of that."

"She wouldn't. Her stepfather Lenny exploited the gift in Dana's mother by having her go on the road to tell fortunes and cast love spells. That didn't sit well with Dana."

"Yeah, I'm sure it didn't, especially after that drunk driver struck and killed her mother at one of those roadside stands." He'd heard about the accident when he was a kid, but he didn't know Dana then. She attended the school at the reservation until she enrolled at Silverhill High.

During their senior year in high school, he believed they'd shared everything about themselves. Apparently not. What other secrets had Dana kept from him?

"Anyway," Emmett continued, "folks on the reservation, who know about Dana's gift, are wondering if she's going to use it to solve these crimes."

"Did you know about this?" Rafe tilted his chin toward Steve, who looked as mystified as Rafe felt. Something else. Fear, like a flame, leaped in Rafe's chest, and he crossed his arms to squelch it.

"Emmett," he began slowly, "does everyone on the reservation know Dana's gifted?"

"Maybe not the younger ones, but the elders all know it because they know the Redbird family has the gift."

Rafe swore and pounded the table with his fist. "You need

to keep that piece of information under wraps as much as you can. If it gets out to the general public that Dana can read minds or see into the future and our killer finds out, she'll be in more danger than ever."

His words hung in the air as the clip of Dana's heels echoed down the hallway. She stopped at the table and rested her hands on the back of her chair.

"I see Emmett's been spinning Native American ghost stories."

Steve said, "Why didn't you tell me you had this gift, Dana?"

She snorted, her nostrils flaring in anger. "I know you have a little Cherokee blood in you, Steve, but do you really believe all that spiritual claptrap?"

"The FBI has used psychics before, and we've gotten some valuable information from them. You should've told me."

"Okay, stop." Dana held up her hands. "I don't have the gift. I've never been able to predict a lottery number, I can't cast spells and I don't see dead people." She lifted one shoulder and said, "I guess it skipped me."

Rafe stood up next to her and grabbed her hand. "Does everyone on the reservation believe that?"

Her eyes widened as she grasped his meaning. "I—I don't know. The Redbirds never made a big deal out of it, except my stepfather. The older folks know, but it's not something I ever discussed…with anyone."

"Don't start now. We don't need this psycho believing you can identify him through dreams." Rafe squeezed her hand, resisting an urge to pull her into an embrace. She'd welcome that about as much as she had welcomed that trip down memory lane.

At least she didn't yank away from him. She briefly leaned against his arm and said, "It's not something I bring up in everyday conversation."

Standing up, Steve unzipped his briefcase and slid his files inside. Without looking up, he asked, "Have you ever tried to use your powers of clairvoyance, Dana?"

She disentangled her hand from Rafe's and smacked it on the table. "I told you, I don't have that ability."

Steve cleared his throat. "From what I understand, it's something you need to develop and practice. You have to make yourself susceptible."

"Well, I'm not making myself susceptible."

"If it could be useful for this case, if it could save some lives?" Emmett shoved to his feet and gripped the edge of the table.

The three of them created a semicircle around Dana. She pulled her shoulders back and widened her stance, but her lower lip trembled. Rafe's protective instincts shot into overdrive.

"Forget it. Dana told you she can't see into the future or read minds. Are you boys so afraid of a little old-fashioned detective work that you have to rely on the mystical dreams of a reluctant psychic?"

Everyone around the table let out a sigh, and Steve rapped his knuckles on the table. "You're right, Sheriff. Dana and I are going out to Holly's house tomorrow. Since her mother was out of town today, I had to give her the bad news over the phone."

Emmett coughed. "And I'm following up on that lead from one of Lindy's coworkers about the customer who kept requesting Lindy's table at the restaurant."

Dana shot him a grateful look from beneath lowered lashes, and Rafe squeezed her hand again.

They stepped outside the station, and Emmett put on his hat and said, "I noticed you drove in with Rafe, Dana. I'm going back out to the reservation. Can I give you a ride back to your auntie Mary's?"

"Sure." She glanced at Rafe. "Thanks for the ride over and..."

"My pleasure." Rafe took her hand, running his thumb across her smooth skin. He knew she wanted to thank him for standing up for her in there and not allowing Steve and Emmett to bully her into using some powers she didn't even think she possessed.

He watched through narrowed eyes as Dana climbed into Emmett's patrol car. It felt natural and right to be Dana's protector again. And if it ever got out that she could identify the killer through supernatural powers, Rafe would do everything in *his* power to shield her from danger.

He didn't have the gift, but he had a gun and he'd go to hell and back to keep Dana Croft safe.

Chapter Three

"Guess who I saw last night?" Rafe shook the container of orange juice with one hand as he took a bite of toast.

His brother, Rod, grunted from behind his newspaper, and his stepmother, Pam, raised her eyebrows as she poured coffee. "Who?" Pam asked.

"Dana Croft."

Rod answered by rustling his paper and cursing. Rafe was pretty sure the curse had nothing to do with Dana. His brother only half listened to what anyone said unless it pertained to the ranch.

Pam responded with a curse, too. She'd poured too much coffee in the cup and the steaming liquid had run over the sides and pooled in the saucer.

Rafe grabbed a dish towel and tossed it to her. "Do you remember Dana? She went off to Georgetown, went to the FBI Academy at Quantico, and now she's working in the FBI's Indian Country Crimes unit. She's in town to investigate those three murders."

Pam's brow furrowed as she dropped the dish towel on the counter to soak up the coffee. "Dana Croft?"

"You remember Dana, Pam." Rod folded his newspaper

and shoved back from the table. "She's the pretty Ute girl you tried so hard to pry away from Rafe during his senior year."

"That's ridiculous." Pam slid the wet towel into the sink. "I never interfered with you boys."

Rafe clenched his jaw as Rod rolled his eyes at him before exiting the pot he had just stirred.

Looked like Dana was right about Pam if Rod had noticed. His stepmother probably told Dana to back off when they were in high school, but the fact that Dana actually did back off shocked the hell out of him. He'd meant it when he told her he never knew her to run from a fight.

Unless the fight concerned something she didn't really want.

Rotating his shoulders, he kicked his boots onto the chair Rod vacated and leaned back. Dana had flitted across his mind a few times in the past several years; why was he allowing her to take up residence now like a big, white elephant in the corner of his brain? Correction. A dark, sleek panther. A sexy cat of a woman.

He gulped his juice. Once they caught this killer and wrapped up the investigation, she'd go back to whatever kind of life she had in Denver. And that suited him just fine. As long as he could keep her safe while she worked the case.

Pam dropped a single rose into the small glass vase on Dad's breakfast tray. Gripping the handles of the tray, she hoisted it from the counter and turned toward Rafe. "You don't believe Rod's nonsense about that girl, do you? With your father's health deteriorating, Rod's had more than he can handle at the ranch. He's always angry about something, and has a sarcastic tongue."

Rafe shrugged. Even at eighteen years old, Dana could stand up to Pam…if she'd wanted to. "That was a long time ago. How's Dad this morning?"

"The flu hit him hard, and it takes him longer and longer to recover from an illness. Doc Parker thinks Ralph needs to retire to a different climate."

Rafe's cell phone rang and he checked the display, which flashed Steve Lubeck's number. His heart skipped a beat. It was too early in the morning for Steve and Dana to have uncovered anything at Holly Thompson's house. He hoped it wasn't another body. "I have to take this."

Pam backed out of the kitchen with the tray almost groaning under the weight of Dad's favorite breakfast. Pam may have broken up his parents' marriage, but she catered to his father in a way his biological mother refused to do. His mother hadn't possessed one nurturing gene in her body. She hadn't contacted one of them since leaving over fifteen years ago.

Shaking his head, Rafe flipped open his phone. "Hey, Steve, anything new?"

"No, unless you count my burning ulcer. I need to see a doctor today. Do you mind going out to the Thompson residence with Dana to talk to Holly's mother? We're supposed to be there at eleven o'clock."

Rafe pulled up his sleeve to check his watch. "Sure. Were you picking up Dana or meeting her there?"

"I was going to swing by her aunt's house to pick her up. The Thompson place is on the other side of the reservation from Dana's aunt's house."

"I'll be there. Did you tell Dana yet?"

"Not yet. Do you want me to call her? I can give her a ring on my way to the doctor in Durango."

"That's okay. I'll call her." Rafe wanted to gauge her response to working with him. His presence seemed to put her on edge, and he planned to find out why.

AFTER THREE UNSUCCESSFUL phone calls to Dana, a three-mile run and a conversation with Alicia Clifton's agitated boyfriend, Rafe pulled into the reservation. His patrol car rolled to a stop behind Dana's rental, and as he opened the door, the wind snatched it from his hand and flung it wide. The winds always kicked up on the reservation. Before the oil money started pouring in, the winds stirred up a lot of dirt from the undeveloped lands. The winds still stirred up dirt, but now it came from the construction sites that dotted the reservation—dumping grounds for a killer.

Rafe's gaze darted toward the thick foliage where Dana's attacker had disappeared last night. One of Emmett's officers had scoured the area this morning, but didn't turn up one clue. The "Headband Killer," as they'd secretly dubbed him, seemed to move about silently and stealthily, snatching women, murdering them and dumping their bodies without leaving a trace of evidence.

Rafe stuffed his hands in his pockets and hunched his shoulders against the sudden chill in the air. If it was their guy who accosted Dana, thank God all he had in mind for her was a warning. But why just a warning? Why didn't he drag her off and strangle her like all the others?

For some reason, despite her Ute heritage, Dana didn't fit his pattern. Or he didn't want to mess with an FBI agent. Or maybe Dana was right—a wannabe attacked her, not the real killer.

He huffed out a breath in the cold air and stomped up the two steps to Mary Redbird's door. Even though she'd married a Croft, everyone called her Mary Redbird or Auntie Mary. After Dana's mother died, her aunt had raised her, since her stepfather, Lenny, was useless. He hadn't been back in town two weeks, and he'd already caused a ruckus at the Elk Ridge Bar the other night.

He knocked on the door and Dana opened it, wearing slacks

and a blouse. This time she had a shoulder holster with her weapon tucked inside, not packed away in her purse.

"What are you doing here?" She grasped the door and the doorjamb, blocking his entrance to the house.

"Steve's ulcer is acting up. I'm going with you to interview Mrs. Thompson."

"Oh, I thought maybe you were just in the neighborhood again."

"I tried calling you on your cell phone a couple of times, but it went straight to voice mail."

"We don't have the best reception out here." Her grip on the doorjamb loosened. "You should've tried my aunt's number."

Rafe jerked his chin forward. "Are you going to invite me inside this time?"

"We need to get going. I'll get my jacket and…"

Auntie Mary ducked beneath Dana's arm. "Nonsense. Come on in, Sheriff McClintock."

Dana's jaw tightened but she threw open the door, and Rafe squeezed past her to clasp Auntie Mary's clawlike hand. "You can call me Rafe, ma'am. You're looking as spry as ever."

Thumping her cane against the floor, Auntie Mary chuckled. "Spry is only ever used for ancient people who haven't dropped dead yet. It's good to see you, Rafe. Haven't seen much of you since you returned to Silverhill, but I did vote for you for sheriff."

"That's good to hear, ma'am. I'm just sorry such sad business brings me to the reservation."

Auntie Mary shook her head. "It's a tragedy for those girls and their families. As much as I like having my great-niece here, I hope you catch this killer quickly."

"We will." His gaze meandered around the cozy living room, settling on the crackling fire in the grate. He stepped toward the fireplace, holding out his hands. "It's chilly outside. I think we're going to have an early winter."

Leaning forward, Rafe peered at the framed photos on the mantel—Dana's high school graduation picture, Dana with the FBI director and several pictures of Dana as a young girl.

He reached forward to pluck one of the photos from the mantel and Dana shouted, "Let's go."

Jerking his head to the side, he almost dropped the frame. "What's your hurry?"

Dana held her breath as Rafe clutched the picture of his daughter, Kelsey, in his hand. She should've seen this coming. The man traipsed around Silverhill, and even the reservation, as if he owned the place. Obviously, he figured he could show up on Auntie Mary's doorstep day or night. She should've insisted Auntie Mary put away all the pictures of Kelsey.

She yanked her suit jacket over her holster. "It's almost eleven. We need to get over to the Thompson house."

Rafe placed the frame back in its place, and Dana let out a slow breath. She needed time to tell him about his daughter, safely at home in Denver with Dana's cousin. She'd wait until the investigation ended because once he found out she'd been keeping this secret for ten years, they'd never be able to work together.

Raising his brows, Rafe glanced at Auntie Mary and she rolled her eyes and said, "You know Dana. Prompt. Punctual."

"Just like you taught me." Dana grabbed her coat from the closet. She had to propel Rafe out of this house—away from the photos, away from the memories.

Rafe turned his back on the fireplace and Kelsey. Dropping an arm around Auntie Mary's shoulders, he bent to kiss her cheek. "We'll catch up another time."

Two circles of color dotted Auntie Mary's cheeks as she

smiled up at Rafe. Dana shook her head. Rafe's easy charm affected all women, young and old. She'd figured out later, after a few psych classes, that the abandonment of his mother drove him to conquer every woman he met.

Did her desertion of Rafe after high school really hurt him like Auntie Mary suggested? He sure seemed to move on quickly.

"Ready?" Dana shrugged into her coat and shrugged off the memories.

Rafe tossed his keys in the air while they walked toward his patrol car. "Do you want to drive over to the Thompson place or walk?"

Normally, she enjoyed a nice, brisk walk, but if Rafe left his car here, they'd have to come back for it and he'd have another excuse to get inside Auntie Mary's house. Dana couldn't allow that. Not with those pictures of Kelsey adorning the mantel.

"It's too cold for a walk." She rubbed her hands together. "And I'm wearing high heels."

"Good point." He jabbed at his remote and opened the passenger door for her, placing his hand on the small of her back. Through her coat, suit jacket and blouse, the man's touch scorched her. When he shut the door, she dragged in a deep breath and whispered, "Get a grip."

He slid onto the driver's seat and cranked on the engine. "Emmett told me one of his guys canvassed the area here this morning but didn't find anything from the attack last night. Have you had any more trouble?"

"No. Emmett had Jimmy patrolling the reservation last night, and I think he made lots of loops around Auntie Mary's place."

"Good. I'm hoping that was our killer. It shows he's cocky, too self-assured. That's going to land him in trouble."

"And if it was the killer who attacked me, he didn't have

murder on his mind. So even though I'm half Southern Ute, I don't fit his profile for whatever reason."

"The first two victims were full-blooded Ute."

"The first two, but not Holly." Dana chewed her bottom lip. "There has to be some other connection."

A few minutes later, Rafe pulled his patrol car in front of the Thompson house. Dana shoved open the car door, grateful for the biting chill in the air. Sitting in close confinement with Rafe did a number on her senses. He didn't even have to turn on the charm for her, his very presence, the timbre of his voice and his clean, masculine scent made her knees weak.

Weak knees—just what she needed for a serial murder investigation.

Rafe pushed open the gate in the front and it banged closed behind them, its latch broken. They climbed up the two steps to the sagging porch and Rafe rapped on the screen door since two pieces of dirty tape crisscrossed the doorbell. Louella Thompson obviously hadn't used the money from the oil wells for home repair.

The door creaked open, and a tall woman, clutching a glass in her hand, peered at them through the screen door. "Sheriff McClintock? I thought the FBI was coming."

"Afternoon, ma'am. One of the agents got sick. I'm his replacement, but I'm with the other agent. Do you remember Dana Croft? Mary Redbird's great-niece?"

"Sure." Mrs. Thompson clicked open the screen door. "I'd heard you were with the FBI, Dana."

"I'm so sorry for your loss, Mrs. Thompson. May we come in and ask you a few questions about Holly?"

Mrs. Thompson nodded and held open the door, ushering them inside. The smell of booze hit Dana like a sledgehammer. It rolled off Mrs. Thompson in waves. She gestured toward a small, plaid sofa. "Have a seat. Do you want a drink?"

Rafe held up a hand. "We're officially on duty, Mrs. Thompson, but thanks anyway."

Dana shooed an orange tabby from the sofa and sank onto the soft, worn cushion. Rafe perched on the edge next to her and swept off his hat.

Mrs. Thompson laughed, a hoarse sound, as if that laugh had been a long time coming. "I'm not offering you the bourbon, Sheriff. That's all mine. I need it now more than ever. Would you like some coffee or water? That's about all I got. How about some hot tea? I have that tea Auntie Mary likes, Dana."

"Nothing for me, thanks."

Dana replied, "I'll have some tea."

Mrs. Thompson lurched toward the kitchen, and Dana pushed up from the sofa. "I'll help."

"You sit down. I need something to keep me busy."

Dana exchanged a look with Rafe. As she settled back on the sofa, she whispered, "Do you think we should come back later? How much help will she be in this condition?"

"Maybe this is the only condition she has. Besides, the alcohol might loosen her tongue, bring down her guard."

Mrs. Thompson appeared in the kitchen doorway, propping her shoulder against the frame. "The kettle's on. What do you want to know about Holly?"

Dana cleared her throat. "Did she have a boyfriend?"

"Holly liked boys…maybe too much." Mrs. Thompson swirled the amber liquid in her glass. "But she didn't have one boy in particular. She dated around like a lot of twenty-one year old girls. Even dated that young sheriff's deputy you have working for you."

A muscle in Rafe's jaw twitched, the only sign that this bit of information surprised him. His stoicism, the mark of a good cop, impressed Dana.

Rafe fished a notepad out of his breast pocket along with a pencil. "Can you give us a list of the guys Holly was seeing, including Brice Kellog? Any of them upset about not having an exclusive relationship with her?"

"Not that I know of."

The teakettle whistled and Mrs. Thompson disappeared back into the kitchen. She called out, "Do you want any sugar?"

"No, thanks." Dana mumbled to Rafe, "I'd better help her with that."

She met Mrs. Thompson at the kitchen door and took the saucer from her unsteady hand. "Why don't you sit down, Mrs. Thompson? Sheriff McClintock left a piece of paper on the table for you to jot down Holly's male friends."

She helped Mrs. Thompson take a seat, placing her glass of liquid comfort on the table in front of her. Balancing her cup and saucer, Dana settled next to Rafe again. She inhaled the fragrant tea before taking a sip. Mrs. Thompson must have gotten the tea from Auntie Mary because it tasted and smelled like her own special blend.

Rafe asked, "Did your daughter seem worried about anything the past few weeks? Did she complain about anyone following or harassing her?"

"My Holly never worried about a thing. She was a high-spirited girl who liked to have fun." Mrs. Thompson sniffled and took another gulp of bourbon.

"Did she keep a diary? Have a computer? Send e-mails to friends?"

"She spent a lot of time on the computer. Would you like to see it? It's in her room."

They followed Mrs. Thompson as she weaved down the short hallway, the cat threading between her ankles. She threw open the door to a small room, crowded with furniture and plastered with posters of tattooed singers and grungy-looking bands.

Dana stepped into the room. The heavy perfume of the wilting roses by the window saturated the air, and Dana massaged her temple against a sudden pain. She hoped her allergy to cats wasn't kicking in.

Photos lined the edge of the dresser mirror, and she bent forward to study the smiling faces. Holly had a lot of friends, and a lot of those friends included men. If they planned to track down all of these guys, they had a huge task in front of them. But they could start with Brice.

Mrs. Thompson backed out of the room. "You two can look around. I'll start working on that list."

Dana noticed her empty glass and figured Mrs. Thompson probably needed a refill, or maybe she just couldn't face her daughter's bedroom.

"Are you surprised that Brice was seeing Holly?"

"Not really, but I'm surprised he didn't mention it. I'll be having a conversation with Brice about his relationship with Holly and about police protocol."

Rafe straddled the chair in front of the computer and brought up Holly's e-mail. "It'll take a while to go through these. I suppose Mrs. Thompson will let us take the computer with us, or we'll get a court order to confiscate it."

"I'm sure she'll let us have it without a court order." Dana flipped up the lid of a small pink box on the dresser and a tiny ballerina sprang to life, spinning to Tchaikovsky. A warm flush spread across Dana's skin, and she lifted the back of her hair and fanned herself. *Where'd that cat go?*

Rafe tapped a few keys on the keyboard and said, "I

wonder if she has one of those My Space pages. Your cyber crimes unit could probably get us a password."

"Mmm." Dana smoothed her palm along Holly's bed-spread, and her hand tingled. *Must be a little static electricity in the room.*

She sat on the edge of the bed and rummaged through the nightstand. Didn't look like Holly kept a diary, but she did have a variety of sex toys and a few condoms. Dana picked up a decorative hairbrush with strands of long, dark hair clinging to the bristles.

Running her fingers across the bristles, she closed her eyes. Her breathing deepened, and Rafe's voice sounded as if it were coming from miles away.

An unseen force jolted her body and her hand curled around the carved handle of the brush as an explosion of lights flared behind her closed eyelids. The roaring in her ears blocked out all her other senses. Her body went rigid and then floated, weightless, timeless.

Then the vision took control of her mind.

Chapter Four

"All these password-protected files are beyond my computer skills, but I'm sure your guys can get in." Rafe clicked the mouse a few times to shut down Holly's computer. He pulled open a desk drawer and grabbed a handful of loose papers and photos. "At least there's no shortage of pictures to study. I don't see any of Brice."

A soft moan brushed the back of his neck, making the hair there stand on end. He jerked his head around and drew his brows over his nose. "What are you doing? Taking a nap?"

Reclining on Holly's jungle-print bedspread, Dana clutched a hairbrush to her chest, her wide eyes staring at the ceiling. Her lips moved as if repeating a phrase over and over, but Rafe couldn't hear any sound.

"Dana!" His voice exploded in the room, but Dana didn't move a muscle except for her mouth forming silent words. Rafe charged to his feet, Holly's papers and memorabilia scattering on the hardwood floor.

He reached the edge of the bed in two steps and clasped Dana's arm, crossed over her chest. Alarm raced through every cell in his body as his fingers tripped across her rigid, cold flesh. Her eyes, directed toward the ceiling, held a vacant look, but they flickered back and forth as if she followed some action only she could see.

A vise gripped Rafe's chest. Was Dana having some kind of seizure? Should he try to move her? Rubbing his hands along her stiff arms, he murmured her name over and over. Her breath, deep and steady, reassured him.

But only for a moment.

She choked and her eyes bulged from their sockets. As Rafe scrambled for his cell phone to call 911, Dana snatched her hands from his, bringing them to her throat. With a wrenching cry, she sat up straight, coughing and sputtering.

Rafe dropped the phone and gripped her shoulders. "Are you all right? What happened? Should I call an ambulance?"

Her gaze cleared and focused on his face. The color ebbed back into her cheeks and she shook her head. "I—I'm fine."

"You were not fine one minute ago." His hand slipped to her back where he rubbed it in little circles. "Did you have an asthma attack or something?"

Although her strange posture and skittering gaze didn't resemble any asthma attack he'd ever seen.

"You were choking. Can you breathe okay?" He skimmed the back of his hand across her cool, dry forehead.

She raised a hand to her slender throat and encircled it with her fingers, a frown marring her smooth skin. "I can breathe just fine."

Dana may be breathing just fine, but his galloping heart had his breath coming out in short spurts. Hunching over, Rafe retrieved his cell phone from the floor. "I'm calling 911."

Her hand shot out and she captured his wrist in a strong grip. "Don't."

He narrowed his eyes while he tapped the phone against his palm. "If you can't tell me what just happened in here, I'm calling you an ambulance. Your body was as stiff as a block of wood, and you were completely unresponsive."

"I'm not exactly sure what happened, Rafe." She closed her eyes and massaged her temples. "I blacked out for a moment."

"Blacked out?" He swallowed hard and slid up his cell. "That's it. I'm calling 911."

Her eyelids flew open. "I blacked out and then I had a vision."

"A vision?" His jaw dropped as an avalanche of questions, thoughts and fears buried him. Feeling like the village idiot, he snapped his mouth shut and shook his head as if to clear it.

Dana nodded slowly, the points of her hair skimming her collarbone. "I had a vision, courtesy of the Redbird family. I've only ever had visions a few times, mostly when I was a child. Before I learned how to suppress them."

She'd just given him the worst possible news. He didn't much relish the idea of Dana Croft traipsing around dead bodies as an FBI agent. He sure as hell didn't want her involved with a serial killer on this level.

He ran a hand through his hair, tugging at the roots, welcoming the pain. "I thought you said the gift passed you by?"

"I lied." She shrugged and rolled off the bed.

Rafe zeroed in on the hairbrush on the middle of Holly's colorful bedspread. He didn't believe in UFOs or Bigfoot, but he'd spent enough time with the Ute tribe and its traditions to have a healthy respect for its culture.

"Did that trigger the vision?" He pointed a surprisingly steady finger at the brush on the bed.

"It was Holly's hair that did it." Dana tucked her own hair behind her ears. "That contact with a part of her opened a gateway for the vision."

"You couldn't suppress it this time?"

Dana dropped her lashes while folding her arms across her

chest. "It's harder to block it when I'm in a highly emotional state myself."

Rafe narrowed his eyes as he studied the curve of Dana's dark lashes and the soft blush that rose to her cheeks. Had his appearance in Silverhill caused her emotions to run high? He'd had the advantage. He knew she was on her way to Silverhill and the reservation. She'd had no warning he'd be here too. Maybe she cared more than she let on with her tough talk.

"Why are you in a highly emotional state?" He raised his brows. Would she finally admit that working together on this case had them both on a roller coaster?

Her eyes widened as she waved her arms around. "Oh, I don't know. Probably has something to do with a serial killer running around the reservation."

She didn't fool him. From what he knew about FBI Agent Dana Croft, she was a professional through and through. But he'd play her game…for now.

He dragged in a deep breath and held it, delaying for a moment the question that had been on his lips since she came out of her trance. The question that could take this investigation in a new direction.

The question that could endanger Dana's life.

"What did you see in your vision?"

"Nothing."

"Nothing? I thought you had an otherworldly moment?"

"I told you, I'm not very good at this clairvoyance crap." She took a spin around the room, her hands shoved in her pockets as if afraid to touch anything else in Holly's bedroom. "I saw a dark shape. I tasted spearmint. I felt a tightness around my throat."

"You were choking." Rafe extended his hand, intent on protecting her from even imaginary madmen.

Ignoring his hand, she raised her shoulders. "That's it. I didn't see anyone's face. I didn't hear anyone's name. We already know the women died by strangulation. Not much use, this vision thing."

"Did you try to block it before it got going, before it could reveal anything?"

"What the hell is that supposed to mean?" Her jaw tightened into a hard line and her dark eyes glittered dangerously.

Rafe pinched the bridge of his nose. When had Dana gotten so prickly? As far as he remembered, their high school romance ended amicably enough. She was the one who broke things off and even though their friendship ended with the romance, he never bore her any ill will. Obviously, she didn't feel the same way. She'd been pushing him away with both hands ever since they reunited over Holly's dead body.

"It doesn't mean anything, Dana. If you tried to suppress a vision of a killer coming at you, I wouldn't blame you one bit. If you're already accustomed to blocking these trances, your mind and body probably kicked into gear."

She sighed, her lower lip trembling, and Rafe had to dig his heels into the floor to keep from going to her and wrapping her up in his arms.

"I suppose I did try to block it. I felt Holly's fear and panic. I didn't want to feel that anymore."

He reached out and rubbed her upper arm. Feeling the tremble ripple through her body, Rafe clasped her hand and her fingers curled around his.

"Are you two finished in here?"

Rafe jumped back from Dana like a teenaged boy caught in his girlfriend's bedroom after school. His gaze darted to Dana's face before shifting back to Mrs. Thompson leaning against the doorjamb, glass in hand.

He didn't want Dana to tell Mrs. Thompson about the vision. He didn't want her to tell anyone.

"She has a lot of stuff on her laptop." Rafe jerked his thumb over his shoulder. "Can we take it and turn it over to the FBI? They can retrieve her e-mails and review any Web sites she visited."

Mrs. Thompson's bloodshot eyes drifted from Rafe's face to the back of Dana's head as she bent over the nightstand drawer to drop the brush back inside.

"Sure. Take it. I got that list on the coffee table." She pointed to the papers scattered on the floor. "Don't leave a mess in here."

"I'd like to take those photos with me if you don't mind." He crouched on the floor to gather up the papers and pictures.

"I don't mind."

"Thank you, Mrs. Thompson. I'll pack up the laptop too, and we'll get out of your way."

Mrs. Thompson pushed away from the doorway, and Dana looked up. She whispered, "Do you think she heard us before?"

"I don't know. She's getting drunker and drunker by the minute. This room's in the back of the house, and we weren't exactly shouting." He walked to the laptop and snapped the lid shut. "You realize the importance of keeping this incident to yourself, don't you?"

"Of course I do. Why do you think I buried my head in the nightstand drawer? But maybe Mrs. Thompson already knows, or at least she was hoping I'd have a vision of her daughter's murder."

"Why do you say that?" Rafe cocked his head while he slipped Holly's laptop into the case he'd found beneath her desk.

"The tea. She offered me some of Auntie Mary's special

blend of tea. Auntie Mary swears that tea relaxes her, making her susceptible to visions."

"And you think Mrs. Thompson gave you the tea to kick start *your* special powers?"

Dana shot a glance at the doorway. "Didn't she have an expectant look in her eyes when she walked in here?"

"How would you know? You never even looked at her."

"Maybe it was her tone of voice. I was afraid she'd see something strange about me."

"There's nothing strange about you, and I don't think she suspected a thing."

Dana nibbled on her bottom lip. "Maybe I do owe it to Mrs. Thompson and all the other families to give it a try, Rafe."

Rafe trained his eyes away from her lips while he massaged her shoulders, her hair tickling the backs of his hands. "I don't think you should be putting yourself in any more danger than you already are investigating this case. Leave it. If the visions come, they come, but don't go seeking trouble."

She briefly laid her cheek against his hand, her touch igniting a fire in his belly. "I guess you're right. The gift never brought anything but trouble to my mom."

He ran his thumb along her jaw. He remembered Dana hated comparisons to her mother. Her mother had died before Rafe met Dana, but he'd heard stories, mostly from Pam, that Ronnie Croft had slept around and couldn't even identify Dana's biological father. Not that Rafe cared.

Dana's refusal to acknowledge she had the gift puzzled Rafe initially. She'd never pushed away her Southern Ute culture before. Now he understood that her reluctance to explore her gift stemmed from the fact that she shared it with her mother. She wanted to distance herself more from her mother than her culture.

Not that he wanted Dana to immerse herself in visions of a serial killer. He'd rather use old-fashioned police work to solve this case than put Dana's life in danger.

She slipped out of his grasp and bent over to smooth the wrinkles from the bedspread with her palms. Her hair hid her expression as it slid across her face. "Grab the laptop and I'll turn it over to Steve. Maybe Holly has something on there that can help us out."

Rafe hitched the laptop case over his shoulder and shoved open the door, gesturing Dana through first. They walked into the living room together where Mrs. Thompson slumped on the sofa, her head tilted back, eyes closed.

A dull pain throbbed at the base of Rafe's skull. He didn't have children, but he couldn't imagine losing a child, especially to murder. When his niece was kidnapped, his brother, Ryder, was almost deranged until he got her back.

Rafe kept his voice low, soothing. "Mrs. Thompson."

Rolling her head to the side, she peeled open one bloodshot eye. "Huh?"

"We're leaving." He patted the side of the laptop case. "Maybe this can tell us something."

She pushed to her feet, swaying slightly. "I'll see you out."

"That's okay. We'll see ourselves out." Dana cupped Mrs. Thompson's elbow.

"I may be drunk, but I haven't lost all my manners." She scooted around the coffee table, banging her shin.

Dana winced, but Mrs. Thompson didn't seem to notice. She shuffled toward the front door and opened it. Standing with her back against the dilapidated screen door, she peered into Dana's face. "Give my best to Mary Redbird. M-maybe she can figure out who's doing this. Maybe she can see who murdered my Holly."

Gasping, Dana drew back. "Auntie Mary doesn't have visions like that, Mrs. Thompson. She's more of a healer."

Mrs. Thompson's hand shot out and grabbed Dana's forearm. "Your mama, Ronnie, had that power. I knew my husband was cheating on me, and Ronnie gave me her name and the name of the hotel where they were meeting. Claimed she saw them there together." Mrs. Thompson tapped her temple. "Up here in her head."

"My mother's dead."

Rafe placed a steadying hand on the curve of Dana's back, feeling a shiver snake through her body. Damn. Maybe Dana nailed it. Maybe Mrs. Thompson suspected some of what went on in Holly's bedroom.

"Don't worry, Mrs. Thompson. We'll get this guy." Rafe stepped between her and Dana and shoved open the screen door. "We'll let you know if we need anything else."

Dana practically flew down the front steps and banged through the flimsy gate. Nothing like acting guilty. If Mrs. Thompson hadn't suspected anything before, Dana's hasty escape might have planted a seed of a notion.

Rafe gave Mrs. Thompson a weak smile and followed Dana out with measured steps. No sense in both of them scrambling from the house.

As Rafe adjusted the broken gate latch, an old Grand Prix lurched to a stop at the curb. A tall, lean man with hard-living lines etched on his face slid from the car and tipped his black cowboy hat in Rafe's direction.

"Afternoon, Sheriff."

Rafe cursed softly and stole a glance at Dana, now frozen beside his squad car. If the vision in Holly's bedroom hadn't already done a number on her nerves, this man with his shifty eyes and sly grin would just about finish her off.

The man flashed that grin at Dana and said, "Well if it isn't my FBI agent stepdaughter. Welcome home, honey."

Dana clenched her hands, her nails digging half circles into her palms. When Auntie Mary told her Lenny had slithered back into town, she knew she couldn't avoid him forever. But this had to be the worst possible time to confront him. Her head still felt foggy from that vision and her knees wobbly from her close encounter with Rafe.

She straightened her shoulders and crossed her arms over her chest. "Lenny."

Tucking a paper bag beneath his arm, Lenny shifted the toothpick in his mouth from one side to the other. "Is that any way to greet your stepfather after all these years? Come on over here and give me a hug, girl. Damn, you're pretty. Just like your mother."

If one more person drew a parallel between her and Mom today, she'd scream. She'd spent a lot of time and effort distancing herself from her mother's haphazard existence, and except for her illegitimate child, she'd been successful. The sooner they solved this case allowing her to get the hell off the reservation, the better.

And what about Rafe?

She shook her head, ridding herself of the whispered words echoing in her head, and then gripped her upper arms. One crisis at a time. She had no intention of giving Lenny Driscoll a hug…now or ever.

"What are you doing here?"

"Didn't Auntie Mary tell you I was in town? I know you haven't been back for a while, but I've been missing in action too. I looked you up once when I was in Denver. Tracked you down and found you at a park, but you were in the middle of some kid's birthday party." His slate gray eyes slid from Dana to Rafe, who had moved to her side and hovered in a protective manner. "I didn't want to bust in on the fun."

Dana's heart flip-flopped. Did Lenny suspect she had a child? He'd store that piece of information and use it when it suited him, when he could gain the most from it.

She ignored his attempts at filial devotion and flicked her hand toward Louella Thompson's house. "I mean what are you doing here, at this particular house?"

As Lenny's eyelids dropped half-mast over his eyes, the lines on his face deepened. "Me and Louella are friends. I'm here to pay my respects."

The screen door banged and Louella propped it open with her shoulder, hugging a sweater to her body. "Hey, Lenny. The sheriff and Dana are done here, come on up."

Lenny drew the paper bag from beneath his arm, clutching the neck of the bottle wrapped inside. He waved it at Louella. "The good stuff."

A hiss escaped between Dana's lips and she pressed them together. *Lenny Driscoll—still doing his best to help women realize their hopes and dreams.*

Dana took one staggering step forward, but Rafe grabbed her hand and murmured, "Leave it alone."

Rafe raised his other hand. "Take care of yourself, Mrs. Thompson. We'll be in touch."

She waved and then slammed the door, shutting herself inside the house with Lenny and a bottle of the good stuff.

Dana sighed while she slumped against Rafe's car. Whenever she saw Lenny, pinpricks of fury needled her skin. Nothing had changed after ten years.

Rafe, his fingers still entwined with hers, tugged her hand. "Are you okay?

"I'm fine." But she still clung to him, wanting to feel his

strength. Rafe had always been the uncomplicated, happy-go-lucky type in high school—no teenage angst for him. That's why Pam's threat had been so successful. Dana hadn't wanted to muck up Rafe's life.

He opened her door and hung on the edge. "If you want, I can take the laptop to Agent Lubeck on my own and you can get some rest."

"Rest?" She snapped on her seat belt. "I don't need to rest after an encounter with my slimy stepfather, although I might need a shower."

"I'm not just talking about Lenny. You sensed Holly's killer today. You felt his hands around your throat. A few more minutes in the trance and you could've looked him in the eyes."

Dana shivered. "But I didn't see him...not this time."

"Will there be a next time?"

Did she detect judgment in Rafe's voice? Did he expect her to make herself susceptible to a killer's mind? To feel the terror of his victims?

And what did she expect from herself?

She had the power to unmask this killer. Her sensitivity exceeded that of her mother and even Auntie Mary. Auntie Mary was the one who taught her how to control and suppress the visions. She'd feared if Lenny discovered Dana's gift, he'd use the child as well as the mother in his quest for money.

Dana had gotten so good at stamping out her clairvoyant abilities, she'd never had to worry about them...until now.

"I'm not suggesting there should be a next time, Dana." Rafe dropped his hand to her shoulder. "I'd be happier if you left it alone."

Could she leave it alone? Being back on the reservation had heightened her senses, and seeing Rafe only made the situation worse. Her proximity to him scrambled her thoughts, weakened her resolve.

Like now. She should be knocking his hand from her shoulder. Shrugging him off. Assuring him she could handle anything.

Instead, she'd tilted her head, brushing the back of his hand with her hair, allowing the warmth of his touch to spread through her body like a salve to her frayed nerves.

She breathed out a soft sigh. "Maybe I don't have a choice, Rafe. Maybe something's headed my way whether I like it or not. And this time I can't stop it, can't run away."

He wedged a finger beneath her chin, tilting her head back. The gaze from his blue eyes burned into hers. "Whatever comes at you, Dana, I'll be right beside you to take it on."

He brushed the whisper of a kiss across her lips before slamming the car door and stalking to the trunk to load Holly's laptop case.

Placing a fingertip on her burning lips, Dana wondered if Rafe realized he posed as great a threat to her as this serial killer.

Chapter Five

"So what happened at Louella's place?" Auntie Mary leaned heavily on her cane and gripped Dana's arm as she hobbled up the two steps to the front of the new Southern Ute Cultural Center.

The smells of freshly cut wood and paint emanated from the front door of the building, and Dana pushed open the door and called, "Ben?" Then she turned to look at her aunt. "I already told you, Auntie Mary. Nothing happened at the Thompsons' house. And really, even if Rafe and I had discovered something, I'm not at liberty to discuss the details of this case with you." She wagged a finger under her great-aunt's nose. "So stop asking."

Dana hadn't yet decided whether or not to allow her gift to take control of her mind and this investigation, and she didn't want to worry Auntie Mary one way or the other.

She peered into the expansive front room of the cultural center and called Ben's name again. Ben Whitecotton, the curator and driving force behind the center, had invited Auntie Mary to preview it before the grand opening later in the week.

Golden shafts of light beamed through the skylights, creating a warm glow in the room and glinting off glass cases containing artifacts from the Ute tribe. Dana breathed, "It's beautiful."

But Auntie Mary wasn't taking in any of it. Her dark eyes drilled into Dana, and the myriad lines on her face deepened. "Something happened out there. You've been agitated ever since Rafe dropped you off. Or maybe it's just being with Rafe again that has you on edge."

"You just don't give up, do you?" Dana dug her fists into her hips. She had to throw Auntie Mary a bone or she'd harass her the rest of the night. "I didn't want to upset you, but I saw Lenny at Louella's house. He arrived just as Rafe and I were leaving."

Auntie Mary's lips tightened for a moment. "He started visiting Louella when he first got back to Silverhill. It took him just a few days to figure out who had oil money and who didn't have a man to share it with."

"Do you mean Lenny's been dating Louella?" Dana raised her brows. "And now she has even fewer people with claims on her oil money."

Auntie Mary drew in a quick breath. "Are you suggesting Lenny had something to do with Holly's murder to lay his hands on Louella's money?"

"I wouldn't put anything past that man, but come to think of it, we haven't even looked at oil money as a motive in these killings."

"Well, I know Lenny and he's capable of evil, but murder's not his style." Auntie Mary shook her head and pulled her shawl around her shoulders.

Dana opened her mouth to protest, but Auntie Mary raised her gnarled hands. "I know you think he had a hand in killing your mother, but you're talking about cold-blooded murder here."

"There's more. He looked me up in Denver and spotted me at a child's birthday party in the park. That was Kelsey's party."

"Do you think he suspects anything?"

"I'm not sure."

"You need to tell Rafe about Kelsey before someone else does."

"Welcome, ladies." Ben Whitecotton had emerged from a doorway in the corner of the room. The heels of his silver-tipped boots tapped against the hardwood floor as he approached them. He spread his arms. "What do you think?"

Gliding toward him, hands outstretched, Dana said, "It's a beautiful space, Ben. The skylights are a wonderful touch."

Ben grabbed her hands and pulled her close for a kiss on the cheek. "It's good to see you again, Dana. I missed you the last time you were here, and you don't come around very often."

She smiled as she shrugged. "My job keeps me busy. It's easier to fly Auntie Mary up to Denver to visit, and my cousin, Jennifer, lives up there too. So she can visit both of us at the same time."

And both of their daughters. Her cousin Jennifer and her husband had a sixteen-year-old daughter, whom Kelsey worshipped, and they were looking after Kelsey while Dana worked this case. But Ben didn't need to know all the details.

"I'm sorry it took a killer to bring you back this time." He flipped his long black ponytail over his shoulder as his lips twisted into a grimace. "You need to stop this guy. I've been working on this beautiful homage to our heritage and just when we're about to open, somebody's running around murdering Ute women."

"We'll stop him. The FBI Indian Country Crimes unit, Emmett and his reservation police department and Sheriff

McClintock and the San Juan County sheriff's department are all on the job."

"Have a lot of faith in Rafe, huh?" He elbowed her gently in the ribs.

Her cheeks warmed, but she pasted a smile on her face. "That was a long time ago."

"I'm just teasing you. Seems a lot of those high school romances failed." Ben glanced at the tips of his boots.

"I heard about your divorce, Ben. I'm sorry. Does Stacey still live in Silverhill?" Ben had married his high school sweetheart, a full-blooded Ute like Ben, but their relationship hadn't worked out any better than hers and Rafe's had.

"No. She moved to New York City...Manhattan."

"Wow, Manhattan's a long way from the reservation."

He shrugged. "She has her life and I have mine. I was just kidding about Rafe. He's a good sheriff, and we're lucky to have him. Now let me give you a tour of the cultural center."

Ben cupped Auntie Mary's elbow as he guided her past the glass cases lining the walls of the front room. Most of the enclosures contained pottery, tools and rock art with pictographs, a specialty of the Ute Tribe. A few of the cases remained empty.

"What's going in here?" Dana tapped the glass of one of the vacant cases.

"Those cases are for some of the more valuable items. They're locked up in the museum in Durango until I finalize the installation of the rest of my security equipment." He put a finger to his lips. "Shh—don't tell anyone we're not completely secure yet. Can you keep a secret, Dana?"

With her heart pounding, Dana glanced at him sideways through lowered lashes. Did everyone in Silverhill suspect she'd been keeping Rafe's daughter from him all these years? Or did the paranoia from years of lying have her in its grip?

She tossed her hair and squared her shoulders. "Are you kidding? That's part of my job description."

Ben laughed and threw open a set of double doors leading to an enclosed patio. Dana recognized the ring of stones painted with bears from her youth. She clapped her hands. "Are you going to stage performances of the Bear Dance?"

"So you remember the old customs." He nodded his approval.

"How could I forget with the living historian here telling me all the stories?" Dana draped an arm around Auntie Mary.

Smiling, Ben patted Auntie Mary's arm. "She helped a lot in my research. So many of the young people have forgotten."

"You obviously haven't."

He tilted his head, his silky ponytail slipping over one shoulder. "It's like you said before. It's part of my job description. Now let me show you the back rooms. We put in a little theater where we're going to show a documentary on the Ute."

When Ben finished his tour, he herded them back into the entrance hall. Dana hugged him. "Thanks for the tour, Ben. I'm looking forward to the opening this weekend."

"Do I get one of those too?"

Dana disentangled herself from Ben and turned toward the door. A tall man with shoulder-length blue-black hair and high cheekbones stood framed by the door.

"Joshua?" Dana covered her mouth with her hand. The good-looking guy at the door had to be Joshua Trujillo, whom she'd known since childhood.

He opened his arms wide. "The one and only."

Dana rushed toward Joshua and threw her arms around him. "I haven't seen you since high school."

"Yeah, big-time FBI agents don't have time to visit the little people." He kissed the top of Dana's head.

Joshua shook hands with Auntie Mary and gave a nod to Ben. "You ready for the big opening this weekend, Ben?"

"Almost."

Ben's eyes narrowed and Dana almost shivered at the cold air between the two men. They'd been good friends in high school.

"What are you doing these days, Joshua? You look fantastic."

"I run a few clubs in Durango, and I'm negotiating to open one in Denver. You'll have to stop in once I get it going."

"Joshua's one of the tribal members who's trying to get the Southern Ute to approve casinos on our land." Ben's thin lips and crossed arms told Dana all she needed to know.

Lifting his shoulders, Joshua smiled. "Calm down, Ben. That's not going to happen now, since the cultural center stands on the very land I wanted for the casino."

"You didn't mention to Dana that one of your clubs in Durango is a topless joint."

Dana's brows shot up. "Really?"

"Oh, come on, Ben. It's an upscale gentlemen's club." Joshua spread his hands and shot a sideways glance at Dana.

Ben dug in his heels. "Dana, do you know Emmett and Rafe talked to Joshua after Lindy's murder because Joshua was interviewing Lindy for a job at his gentlemen's club?"

"Damn it, Ben. They didn't pursue that lead—nothing to it." Joshua turned his back on Ben. "Have you seen Rafe yet, Dana? I should hold a grudge against the man since he stole my girl."

Dana's cheeks warmed. She and Joshua had been close before they both went to Silverhill High, but she wouldn't call their relationship a romance. Did Emmett even have his interview with Joshua in his case file? If so, she'd missed it. "Of course I've seen Rafe. We're working together."

"I had you all to myself on the reservation. Then when we

went to Silverhill High, all the white boys dazzled you." Joshua's eyes glittered, and his smile bared his teeth.

Dana's blood heated, her face growing hotter…and probably redder. "That's crap, Joshua. Maybe I just sensed then that you had a fondness for exploiting women."

Joshua's sharp laugh echoed in the expansive room. "You and Ben. Hey, if women want to remove their tops and shake it a little for some extra cash, I'm just giving them the opportunity. And you're right. Only one white boy dazzled you."

She snorted. "Just keep believing we would've been together if it hadn't been for Rafe."

Although Joshua was right about the dazzling part. Once she'd met Rafe, she couldn't see anyone else, but it had nothing to do with his skin color.

"Is this trip about second chances?" Joshua winked. "Because if it is, I'm in the running."

Dana shook her head. What happened to the shy, sensitive boy she knew? "This trip is about a murder investigation. You should realize that since you knew most of the victims."

She had backed away from Joshua during the conversation, and now Ben rubbed her back. "I think you should get Mary Redbird home. She looks tired, and Joshua and I have a little business to discuss."

"Really?" Dana put her arm around Auntie Mary and led her to the door, past a smirking Joshua. "I thought the casino idea was dead in the water."

"It's not about that." Ben rubbed his hands together. "Joshua has something I want."

Dana shrugged and left the two men to their business. Ben had given them a thorough and interesting tour of the cultural center, but Auntie Mary looked tired and Dana's grumbling stomach reminded her that she hadn't eaten since grabbing a quick sandwich at Steve's hotel when she and Rafe had turned over Holly's computer. Steve planned to turn it over to the FBI's cyber crimes unit for further analysis.

When they arrived at Auntie Mary's house, Dana settled her aunt in a chair by the fireplace and tucked her shawl around her.

"Put your feet up. I'll heat some of the leftover chili and make you a sandwich. Is that enough?"

"That's more than enough. Just the chili for me. Now let's get back to that conversation Ben interrupted."

Suppressing a sigh, Dana ducked her head into the fridge to rummage for the chili. Auntie Mary had dozed during the ride back to her house, and Dana had hoped she'd forgotten about Lenny and his veiled threat. She shouldn't have mentioned it at all, but she'd wanted to divert her aunt's curiosity from what had happened in Holly's bedroom. Once you started keeping secrets, it became a never-ending labyrinth.

She placed the plastic bowl in the microwave and slammed the door. "It's interesting that Lenny was seeing Louella before her daughter was murdered, and you can bet we're going to look into it further. I'm also going to ask Emmett and Rafe about Joshua's topless club. I wonder if the other women had any connection to him. Wow, he sure has changed."

"I'm not talking about all that, and you know it. Stop trying to change the subject."

Dana folded her arms and rested her hip against the back of the sofa. "I probably imagined that Lenny suspected something about Kelsey."

"Whether he suspects anything or not isn't the point. When are you going to tell that fine man he has a nine-year-old daughter?"

Dana twisted her hands, her ring cutting into her palm. She

deserved the pain, welcomed it. She'd allowed the deception to go on for too long. Rafe would never forgive her now. He had a right to know about his daughter. Her lies to Kelsey had spun out of control too. Her daughter had grandparents, uncles and now an aunt and a cousin.

She was a McClintock.

"Tell him before someone else does, Dana. And you'd better have a good explanation as to why you kept his daughter from him all these years."

Dana covered her face with her hands and took a turn about the small room. "You know why I didn't tell him about the pregnancy. Pam warned me if I told Rafe about my pregnancy, his father would disinherit him, banish him from the family."

"Do you really think Ralph McClintock would cut off one of his sons? And for what, bringing another McClintock into the world?"

"I didn't want to take that chance. Rafe had already lost his mother. I didn't want to be responsible for wrenching him away from the rest of his family."

"You don't know Ralph McClintock. Years ago, a rumor was circulating that Ralph got one of those ski instructors pregnant and planned to take the baby from her and raise it with that wife of his. Probably another reason Rafe's mother escaped from the marriage. Ralph McClintock is interested in more McClintocks. Period."

"It wasn't just that. You know what everyone would've said—she's just like her mother, just like Ronnie Croft."

Auntie Mary quirked an eyebrow. "Everyone would have said that or just Pam McClintock…just you?"

"Everyone." Dana dashed a tear from her cheek. Auntie Mary didn't know what it was like to be thrust into the high school in Silverhill after living on the reservation. She'd always lived on Ute land, respected and revered by everyone on and off the reservation. The white kids at the school expected the kids from the reservation to fail—to drink, to get high, to get pregnant. Dana never wanted to give them that satisfaction.

And she hadn't wanted to ruin Rafe's life, saddle him with a girlfriend and a baby he didn't want, perhaps at the expense of his McClintock family roots.

"Pam was right. It would've destroyed Rafe's life. I did it for him."

"Kelsey didn't destroy your life."

Dana's lip trembled. No, she'd never thought of Kelsey as a mistake. But Rafe wouldn't have felt that way, especially if his father had disinherited him. Rafe had gone off to college in California. He became a cop in L.A. He had goals and plans, and a baby didn't fit into his scenario. He wanted to move to California, and she had a full scholarship to Georgetown. She wasn't going to give that up.

She gasped and clutched her sweater around her throat.

She didn't want to be humiliated. *She* didn't want to give up her scholarship. *She* didn't want to give up her dreams.

What about what Rafe wanted? She'd never given him a chance to find out. The pregnancy and the decisions that followed revolved around her and her desperate need to distance herself from a mother who used her body and then her sacred Ute powers for financial gain.

Dana never wanted any part of that. Somehow Pam McClintock knew it and exploited Dana's fears, throwing in that part about Ralph banishing Rafe from the family for good measure.

She sank onto the sofa across from Auntie Mary. "I know I was selfish to keep the pregnancy a secret from Rafe. When his stepmother found out about the pregnancy, she confronted me. She used it to break up our relationship."

Auntie Mary hunched her shoulders. "Rafe never did listen much to Pam. I don't think she would've had much influence with him."

"Maybe not, but she used the opportunity to tell me all about Mom." Dana sawed at her bottom lip. Did Auntie Mary even know all of Ronnie's dirty little secrets?

Folding her hands in her lap, she scooped in a deep breath. "Pam told me Mom slept around and specifically targeted the rich ranching families, the Pierces, the Prices, the Scotts… even Ralph McClintock, although Pam assured me she never got far with Ralph. When Mom got pregnant with me, she used it to try to coerce these men into marriage."

Dana snuck a tear-blurred glance at Auntie Mary, whose dark eyes shimmered with her own unshed tears.

Dana drew a shuddering breath. "They all refused and denied fathering her child. Mom told me Jack Pierce was my father, but after Pam's story I couldn't believe that anymore. Jack never recognized or acknowledged me all the years he lived in Silverhill."

Auntie Mary nodded her head, a single tear rolling down her creviced cheek. "Ronnie was always insecure. She was a beautiful girl, but she never felt she was good enough. You're beautiful too, Dana, but you developed your mind. You're strong and confident and nothing at all like your mother."

"S-so you knew all about Mom and her plans to marry rich?"

"Of course, but I couldn't do anything to stop her. She was headstrong, and that is a quality you share with her."

"Do you understand why I couldn't tell Rafe about the pregnancy? It was like history repeating itself with Ronnie Croft's daughter—only the daughter landed the big fish…a McClintock. Pam threatened to tell Rafe all about my mother and suggest that I had the same plan to ensnare him into marriage."

Dana stretched out her arms, palms up, asking her aunt to understand, trying to understand herself.

"I can see how that threat would work on a frightened, confused eighteen-year-old girl, especially a girl like you, a girl who had something to prove. But you're not that girl anymore. You're a successful, strong woman with a child who needs her father."

"You're right." Dana slumped against the cushions. "I have to tell him. He'll hate me. He'll never forgive me. He grew up in that household of secrets and lies before his mother deserted the family, and he loathes deception in anyone."

"That's the price you have to pay. Rafe may surprise you. I'm sure he's made mistakes too."

The microwave buzzer had sounded several minutes ago, so Dana pushed up from the sofa. She ladled steaming chili into two bowls and carried them to the living room.

As she placed Auntie Mary's bowl on a tray in her lap, she asked, "So is Jack Pierce my father or not?"

"I don't think so." Auntie Mary blew on a spoonful of chili. "I think your father is Ennis Price's boy, Jonah Price. I think your mother knew it, but Jonah was a wanderer and a gambler—not husband material. I don't think old Ennis even left the ranch to him. It's still vacant, waiting for the granddaughter or something…the legitimate granddaughter."

Dana shoved the spoon into her mouth, burning her tongue on the chili. She could be crazy Ennis Price's granddaughter. Did she want her own daughter to grow up like that? Not knowing her father? Not knowing her family? She had to find a way to tell Rafe about Kelsey.

Later that night, Dana lay awake in bed watching the digital clock click from twelve minutes past midnight to thirteen minutes past midnight. The day's events raced through her head—the vision, bumping into Lenny and then Joshua, the emotionally charged conversation with Auntie Mary.

And beneath the jumble of thoughts lay one constant…her feelings for Rafe. After all these years, those hadn't changed. One look from him, one touch, one kiss turned her insides to jelly. She still wanted him. He still wanted her.

But her deception ensured she'd never have him.

The phone on the nightstand rang, sending a shrill sound through the quiet house. Adrenaline coursed through Dana's body.

A call after midnight always meant bad news.

Chapter Six

Rafe rubbed his eyes as he peered into the darkness cloaking the highway, watching for a pair of headlights. He hadn't wanted Steve to call Dana, to wake her up and drag her out to another murder site. Of course, he never made that ridiculous request. Steve and Emmett would question his sanity and Dana would scorn his efforts to protect her…an experienced FBI agent doing her job.

Worry had gnawed at his gut all day. Dana's vision scared the hell out of him, and the fact that Louella Thompson might have shared her suspicions about Dana with Lenny heightened his concern. Lenny could use the information to blackmail Dana or even worse. He could spread it around the reservation and Silverhill, painting a target on Dana's back.

Two beams of light swept around the corner and barreled toward the parking lot of the new Shopco, already crowded with cop cars, a few reporters and two ambulances. The car squealed to a stop and Dana flung open the door and strode to the center of the action, her long, denim-clad stride eating up the space between them.

Rafe snorted. She hardly looked like a woman in need of protection.

She joined the group of men and hooked her thumbs in the front pockets of her jeans. "What do we have?"

Steve answered his partner. "Like I told you on the phone, Dana, it looks like it's another Headband slaying."

"Dumped in a parking lot? Or did we get lucky and hit on the scene of the murder?"

"We got lucky in a couple of respects." Emmett scratched his jaw and nodded toward the body. "He murdered her here in the parking lot, and a couple of teenagers saw him drive away."

Dana gasped. "Do we have a make, model or license on the vehicle?"

"Not that lucky." Rafe hated to be the one to disappoint her...again. "The teens drove up and parked, facing west. They noticed two cars in the parking lot when they arrived, but figured they were vacant or contained other teens on a midnight tryst. Then they got down to business and looked up only when they heard one of the cars drive away."

"The kids discovered the body?" Dana glanced at the two teenagers sitting on the back end of one of the ambulances. "That's rough."

The boy had his arms wrapped around the girl who sobbed against his shoulder. Rafe's gaze lingered on the couple. He knew them both—the star of the boys' basketball team and a Native American girl who had won a scholarship to a space camp in Houston last summer. Reminded him of two other naive high school kids.

He blinked and slid his gaze to Dana's face, but she had her eyes locked on the dead girl crumpled next to her car in the parking lot.

"Who is she?"

"Jacey Holloway." Emmett whipped a handkerchief out of

his pocket and mopped his face, despite the chill in the air. "She's half Ute. She must've driven out here to meet someone. She doesn't work at Shopco and the store's been closed for over four hours."

Dana edged toward Jacey's lifeless body as the FBI's fingerprint guys finished dusting the car and Jacey's purse, still sitting on the passenger seat. She pointed to the girl's head. "She's not wearing a bandana and feather."

Steve knelt next to the body. "He must add that charming touch when he dumps them." His gloved finger swept along the angry red marks on Jacey's throat.

"Strangled like the others. And look at this." His fingertip traced a red blotch near the girl's collarbone.

Frowning, Rafe bent down for a closer look. "That's consistent with a similar mark on Holly's neck. Jewelry? A ring?"

"Looks like it." Dana bent forward, putting her hands behind her back.

Was she afraid to touch Jacey's body? What would the dead girl tell her? Could Dana glean enough information from her vision to give them a lead on this guy?

Rafe clenched his jaw. He had no business judging Dana. Hell, just watching her in that trance today freaked him out. It must have terrified her.

Running a hand through his hair, Rafe stepped back and grabbed the edge of the car door. "Anyone check Jacey's purse yet?"

Steve answered, "No. They just finished the fingerprints."

Rafe pulled a pair of gloves out of his jacket pocket and slipped them on, wiggling his fingers into the ends. He unzipped Jacey's purse and dumped the contents on the seat. He flipped open her wallet containing her driver's license, a few credit cards and a small amount of cash. Her pink cell phone reflected the glow from the dome light, and Rafe pinched it between his thumb and forefinger and slid it open.

"Any messages?" Dana peered over his shoulder, her warm breath a whisper against his ear.

Rafe squinted at the small screen of the phone. "No voice mail messages, but she has eight text messages."

"Let's read them." In her eagerness, Dana reached forward and pressed the message button. Several messages scrolled onto the screen, and Rafe held the phone under the light to read them.

"Damn." Rafe rubbed his eyes as if to erase the words that floated before him on the cell phone display.

"What is it?" Her hair tickled his cheek. Any other time, any other place, he would've welcomed the sensation. But even being in close proximity to Dana Croft couldn't soothe the pounding drumbeat in his temples.

He tapped the phone, and Dana snatched it from his hand. "Brice? Oh, my God. Is this *your* Brice?"

"I don't know any other Brice in town." He could barely form the words in his dry mouth. If one of his men was involved in this…

"Did you find something?" Emmett ducked his head in the other side of the car.

"A text message from Brice Kellog on Jacey's phone." Rafe held out his hand for the cell phone and Dana dropped it into his gloved palm.

Emmett swore. "You're kidding. What's it say?"

Rafe cleared his throat. "Meet me at the Shopco at midnight."

"Is he on duty tonight?" Emmett's narrowed gaze scanned the law enforcement personnel scattered across the Shopco parking lot.

"Nope. He's off." Rafe scratched the stubble on his chin. "There's something else, Emmett. When Dana and I were at

Holly Thompson's house today, her mother told us Holly dated Brice once or twice. Since he was off today, I'd planned to talk to him about it tomorrow…today."

"Sounds like we need to talk to him now. Do you think he lured her out here and killed her? What about the other girls? We need to put a rush on Holly's phone records." Emmett slammed the roof of the car.

"Hold on, Emmett." Rafe edged around to Emmett's side of the car and Dana followed close on his heels. "Let's talk to the guy first. We can't try and convict him on one text message."

Emmett ran his fingers along the rim of his hat. "I know that, Rafe, but this is the best lead we've had so far."

Rafe's eyes flicked to Dana's face, which appeared pale in the sweeping spotlights that illuminated the crime scene. Of course, Emmett didn't know about the other potential lead that occurred in Holly Thompson's bedroom. And Rafe had no intention of telling him.

"I'm going out to his place to talk to him right now."

Her eyes wide, Dana tugged at the sleeve of his jacket. "I'm coming with you."

Did she hope to pick up some vibes from Brice, or did she want to escape the vibes from the murder scene? Either way, he wanted her company…anyway he could get it.

The three agencies held a quick meeting to review the possible evidence left in the parking lot, and then Rafe bundled Dana into his squad car for the drive to Brice's place in Silverhill.

He slid his gaze to her face, shadowed in the dark car. "What are you thinking? Did you feel anything back there?"

"Yeah, I did." She leaned her forehead against the window and her hair fell across her face. "She called out to me, Rafe."

"What?" He nearly ran off the road as a chill snaked up his spine. "Jacey?"

"It's not like I heard voices, but some force was pulling me toward her, willing me to touch her hair, her skin, compelling me to divine her secrets."

"So why didn't you?" Rafe clutched the steering wheel so hard his knuckles cracked.

She hunched her shoulders. "I'm a coward."

"The hell you are." He smacked the console. "Nobody's going to call you a coward for refusing to lay your hands on a dead body."

Sighing, she leaned her head against the headrest and closed her eyes. "That's why I wanted to come with you to interview Brice."

"To escape the voices?"

"To see if you could get him to confess so I don't have to explore my gift."

"Even if Brice doesn't confess to anything more than an illiterate text message, you don't have to go down that road, Dana." He ran his palm along her thigh, the worn denim of her jeans soft to his touch. Her muscles tensed beneath his hand and he gave her knee a little squeeze before releasing her.

He understood her conflict over the situation. She had an opportunity to glean some information about a killer by using powers she'd rejected years ago. Those powers frightened her, but the fear she felt while in a trance rivaled the disgust she felt at being linked to her mother. That's the last thing Dana wanted.

"I may have to go down that road…for those girls."

She pushed her fingers through her hair, barely resembling the sleek style from earlier today. That midnight call had yanked her out of bed, and she'd pulled on a pair of old jeans and stuffed her feet into some fur-lined boots. She didn't have a drop of makeup on her face either, and she still took his breath away.

His fingers itched to soothe the worry lines from between her eyebrows. His arms ached with a need to hold her close and whisper words of comfort in her ear. His lips…okay, he'd stop right there.

He swung into Brice's driveway with dread pounding at his temples. He'd encountered a few cases of dirty cops in L.A., but murder? He refused to believe he'd been that wrong about Brice, but some people kept secrets as easily as pulling on a pair of pants in the morning.

He cut the engine as he glanced at Dana's profile. That's what he'd liked so much about Dana. No secrets. When Emmett blurted out the truth about Dana's heritage from the Redbird family, it shocked Rafe—not that she had the gift, but that she'd kept it from him. He knew she had her reasons, and he could understand the deception and forgive her.

He could forgive her just about anything.

Letting out a long breath, Rafe surveyed the area. No car in sight, but he knew Brice kept his Mustang in the garage. Surely the kids in the parking lot would've noticed a souped-up car like Brice's pulling out. The noise from his engine could wake the dead. Almost.

"Okay, let's do this." Dana popped open the car door. "Do you want me to take the lead since he's your guy?"

"I can handle Brice."

They strode up the porch together and Rafe banged on the front door. "Brice, it's Rafe. Open up."

He punched the doorbell several times and pounded again. The porch light flicked on, bathing them in a waxy glow. The scraping noises of the dead bolt indicated Brice was fumbling with the key. Did they wake him, or was he putting on an act?

The door inched open, and one sleepy eye appeared in the crack. "What the hell is going on?"

"I need to talk to you. Let us in." Rafe would save the news about the murder until he stood toe-to-toe with Brice and could gauge his reaction.

"What time is it?" Brice swung open the door, but still blocked their entrance.

"Are you going to make us stand out here the rest of the morning?"

"Us?" Brice rubbed his eyes and yawned.

If this was an act, he was putting on a damned good show. Rafe stepped to the side to reveal Dana perched on the bottom step.

Brice gulped and backed up. "Let me get some pants on."

As he walked away, Rafe could see that he'd put his boxers on backward. Brice stumbled into the hallway and Rafe raised his brows at Dana, closing the door behind them.

He whispered, "What do you think?"

She shrugged. "Looks like he just woke up and pulled on his underwear…backward."

A door clicked shut and Brice came from the back of the house, buttoning his fly. "Sorry, Agent Croft. Now, what's this all about, Sheriff? Has there been another murder?"

"Now why would you say that?"

"Are you kidding?" Brice rubbed a hand over his rumpled hair. "We have a maniac out there killing girls and you're banging on my front door with the FBI at—" he squinted at the clock on the kitchen wall "—two o'clock in the morning on my day off…or what used to be my day off."

"Yeah, there's been another murder. Where were you three hours ago?" Rafe crossed his arms and clenched his jaw. *Give me a good answer, buddy.*

Brice's eyes widened as his gaze darted between Rafe and Dana. "Me? You're asking me for an alibi? Who was it?"

"Jacey Holloway." Dana shoved her hands in her pockets. "You know her, Brice?"

Brice swore and sank to the sofa, burying his head in his hands. As his shoulders shook, Rafe exchanged a glance with Dana. If Brice did kill Jacey, he could give Al Pacino a run for his money.

Rafe cleared his throat. "Brice?"

Brice raised his head, the heels of his hands pressed to his eyes. "God, not Jacey."

"Did you know Jacey?" Dana sat on the sofa next to Brice and touched his shoulder. "Were you dating her?"

"Not yet." He sniffled and rubbed a hand beneath his nose. "We hooked up a few weeks ago. I got her number, and we were going to try to hook up again."

"Did you text her tonight?" Rafe narrowed his eyes, watching for a sign or a slipup.

Brice's mouth hung open while his head jerked between Dana and Rafe. "Tonight? No, I didn't text her tonight."

"Well, that's the problem, Brice." Rafe hooked his thumbs in his belt loops, lifting his shoulders. "We found a text message from you on Jacey's cell phone—a message asking her to meet you in the Shopco parking lot…the same parking lot where someone strangled her."

Brice bounded from the sofa and cursed. "I did not text Jacey tonight." He lunged across the room and whipped his jacket off the back of a kitchen chair. He grabbed one pocket and then the other and cursed again.

"I thought I left my cell phone in my pocket." He pointed to a door that led to the garage. "Can I check my car?"

Rafe nodded and sauntered to the garage door to follow

Brice. Brice stuck his head in the Mustang and called back over his shoulder, "It's gone."

He followed Rafe back into the house, rubbing his bare arms. "Someone must've stolen it and then used it to text Jacey."

"Or you sent Jacey that text message, murdered her and then tossed the phone out so you could claim somebody stole it." Dana had her finger leveled at Brice, and his mouth gaped open like a fish on a hook.

"Why didn't you tell me you were dating Holly Thompson?"

Brice swiveled his head back toward Rafe. "I—I was going to tell you that, Sheriff, but we weren't really dating. We just…ah…slept together a few times."

"And you didn't think that was important information for a murder investigation?"

Clutching his hair, Brice paced the floor. "Yeah, I knew it was. I swear I was going to tell you."

"By not bringing it up first, you put yourself in a mighty awkward position, especially for an officer of the law. Thought I trained you better than that, Brice."

"I swear, Sheriff, I had nothing to do with the murders. Someone stole my phone or I dropped it. I'll take a lie detector test…anything…"

Dana interrupted his babbling by slicing her hand through the air. "First you need to tell us where you were tonight, Brice."

His Adam's apple bobbed. "I was at the Elk Ridge Bar. I left around ten-thirty."

"Where did you go?" Dana had taken out a pad of paper and a pen. Despite her casual clothes, she radiated a no-nonsense professionalism.

"I came home."

"Alone?" Dana's gaze drifted toward the darkened hallway.

Brice took a deep breath and squared his shoulders. "Yes."

A woman's voice floated from the back. "Oh, honey, you don't have to lie for me. This is too serious."

Belinda Mathers, very rich and very married and wrapped in the khaki shirt from Brice's uniform, sashayed into the living room.

"Hello, Sheriff McClintock." Her gaze raked him up and down, and with it he felt his clothing peel away.

"Belinda." He shifted his hat in front of his crotch. "How long have you been here with Brice?"

She grinned while her eyes dropped to his hat. "All night long, Sheriff. We met up at the Elk, and I saw him use his cell phone about a half hour before we left…together. He was calling a friend to let him know he wouldn't be going to another club in Durango. If someone used Brice's cell phone to send a message to that poor little girl, he must've stolen it from Brice or found it in the parking lot of the Elk. That's where you should be looking."

"You don't have to do this, Belinda." Brice held out his hand to the woman, who had a good twenty years on him and a hell of a lot of experience.

She laughed, a husky sound, and then reached up and fluffed her hair. "Don't worry, honey. My husband's used to it."

Dana coughed. "Did you leave your jacket unattended at the Elk? Could someone have stolen the phone from the bar?"

"I suppose so."

"Aren't you Ronnie's girl?" Belinda squinted at Dana. "Now there's a woman who knew how to have a good time."

Rafe rolled his eyes at Dana, trying to make a joke out of it. Dana's eyes glittered as she turned her back on Belinda and faced Brice.

"Did anyone know you'd hooked up with Jacey?"

Brice choked out, "Do you think someone's trying to frame me? I mean, first Holly and then Jacey."

"What about Lindy and Alicia?" Rafe's heart thumped in his chest. Could his own deputy be the link all these girls shared?

"I saw Lindy around at some of the bars and clubs in Durango, and I knew Alicia's boyfriend, but I never…ah… dated either one of them."

Rafe let out a long sigh, but they still had the cell phone. Brice made a call from the Elk around ten o'clock, and then someone used the same phone to send a text message to Jacey at eleven-twenty. That placed the killer at a general time and a specific location.

Relieved his deputy didn't have anything to do with the murders, Rafe gripped his hand in a firm shake. "We'll need to go back to the Elk tomorrow, retrace your steps, talk to the bartender. We've got ourselves a break."

Brice returned his grip. "I'll be there, Sheriff, and I'm sorry I didn't come clean before about Holly." Brice passed his hands over his face. "I can't believe this is happening to those girls."

"C'mon, honey." Belinda crooked her index finger. "I'll make it all better." She prowled back toward the bedroom, her shapely hips swaying suggestively.

Brice opened the door for Rafe and Dana. "I'll be at the station in a few hours."

"See you then." Rafe smacked the doorjamb with the palm of his hand. "Get some sleep and…try to keep your pants on."

When Rafe slid into the front seat of his squad car, he whistled. "I'm glad Brice was boinking Belinda Mathers instead of murdering Jacey Holloway."

Dana snorted. "When you mentioned Brice had a thing for the ladies, you weren't kidding. For a minute there, I thought our killer might be some disgruntled husband or jealous suitor who had it in for lover boy there."

Rafe snapped his fingers. "Hey, that's not a bad theory. Maybe we need to look a little more closely at Alicia's boyfriend, Patrick Rainwater. Brice said he knew Alicia's boyfriend. Maybe Patrick got jealous."

"But Alicia wasn't the first victim. Why would he kill Lindy? Brice said he didn't even know Lindy."

"I'm just grasping at straws. It's late. I'm punchy."

"And you need to drive me back to the Shopco parking lot. My car's still there. Sorry." Her fingers danced along his knuckles.

"I can take you to Auntie Mary's and then get you out to Shopco tomorrow morning." *Or I can take you back to the guesthouse on the ranch and make hot, sweet love to you all night long.*

Her touch had ignited a fire in his belly, giving him crazy thoughts. He slanted a gaze her way to see if she noticed his pounding heart.

"That's out of your way. You need to be at the station tomorrow morning, and I need to meet Steve at his hotel. We have a conference with the Bureau in Denver." She stretched out her legs, tilted back the seat and closed her eyes.

Nope. She didn't have a clue about his pounding heart or any other part of his anatomy.

They drove in silence until they hit the Shopco parking lot. The police and FBI had deserted the crime scene, leaving four cones set up in a square with yellow police tape attached, which outlined the immediate crime scene. The authorities had already towed away Jacey's car and Emmett's guys would comb through it again tomorrow for any more evidence.

The dark asphalt yawned in front of them, empty except

for two cars they'd already checked out and cleared and Dana's rental. Rafe pulled up next to Dana's car.

Her eyelids flew open as she hugged her purse to her chest. "We're here already?"

Rafe pushed open his door, ambled around to her side and opened the passenger door for her. She licked her lips and then unfolded her legs, exiting the car.

After the earlier commotion and lights, an eerie hush had settled over the parking lot. Hunching her shoulders, Dana gripped her upper arms.

Rafe hooked an arm around her waist, pulling her close. She rested her head against his chest while he smoothed her hair back from her face. She shivered and he wrapped his arms around her, inhaling her faded perfume like flowers crushed in a book.

Weaving one hand through her silky hair, he gently pulled her head back, tilting her face toward his. Her ripe lips parted and that's all the invitation he needed. He possessed her mouth with his own with a fierceness that had been building since the moment he caught sight of her.

Her spine stiffened against his assault, and then her body arched against his, making contact along every line of his frame. Her lips moved beneath his kiss, her teeth nipping his lower lip as if to stake out her own claim.

She entwined her arms around his neck, digging her fingernails into his shoulders. Punishing him for wanting her. Just like she punished him for loving her all those years ago.

What had he done to make her run away? What excuse did any woman need to run away from Rafe McClintock, shallow party boy? He'd always been unlovable. Good for the short term but not much else.

Dana dropped her arms and stepped back. "What's wrong?"

Rafe sucked in a breath. He hadn't realized he'd stopped stroking her hair, stopped kissing her. "Nothing…I…"

"You're right." She shook her head, waving her hands in front of her. "Someone committed a murder here over four hours ago, and we're standing in almost the same spot making out. Stress does funny things to people."

Shoving his hands in his pockets, Rafe dropped his head. Nobody messed with his mind the way Dana did. God, he'd never win her back by playing the morose, moody cowboy. Women didn't want depth from him. They wanted a good time.

"Will you be okay to drive back to Auntie Mary's?"

She smiled a little too brightly. "Of course."

"I'll check on you later." He lifted his hand in a wave and slid onto the driver's seat of the car.

He hardened his jaw as he watched her climb into her rental. He had to have it out with her. He had to discover why she had broken it off. Had to discover why she had left him. Had to discover why she had stayed away all these years.

Even if the discovery killed him.

Chapter Seven

"Idiot." Dana spit out the word between clenched teeth as she pasted a phony smile on her face and waved at Rafe. Why had she chosen that particular time and place to succumb to her gooey feelings for the man? A crime scene didn't give most women romantic thoughts. He probably pushed her away because he pegged her as some kind of weirdo or thrill-seeking junkie.

She waited until Rafe started his engine before she pulled forward, the comforting sight of his headlights behind her. The murder, the disturbing aura of the parking lot, the questioning of Brice and, yeah, Belinda Mathers's comment about Ronnie had chipped away at her resistance all night.

When Rafe took her in his arms, all resolve melted. She still wanted him…but she could never have him. Not once he discovered she'd been keeping his child from him. Could he forgive her? Would he believe she only wanted to protect him? Would he understand her shame that despite her best efforts, she'd ended up just like her mother after all?

"Weak, Dana," she scolded herself aloud. What about all those intervening years? She'd graduated summa cum laude from Georgetown and finished near the top of her class at the

FBI Academy. Her life bore no resemblance to Ronnie's ramshackle existence, and Rafe was well out of his father's sphere of influence by then.

She'd kept loose tabs on Rafe's life after Silverhill. She knew he'd moved to L.A. and lived the life of a carefree bachelor. A few of his buddies he'd kept in touch with had repeated some of his exploits in L.A. in tones of reverence and with a touch of envy. After hearing the stories, she hadn't wanted to torpedo his glamorous lifestyle.

"Pride." She jumped at the sound of her own voice. Her mother didn't have enough pride, and Dana overcompensated for that weakness by stuffing herself full of the seventh deadly sin.

She pulled up to the stop sign and beeped her horn once as she made the left turn toward the reservation. Rafe peeled away from her, heading north toward the center of Silverhill and the McClintock ranch.

She peered at the stretch of road illuminated by her headlights while she chewed on her bottom lip. She had to tell him about Kelsey before she left Silverhill. She'd wait until they caught the Headband Killer to avoid the distraction.

She snorted. Rafe would view the fact that he had a nine-year-old daughter as more than a distraction.

Several miles later, her headlights picked out a dark shape in the road and Dana laid on her horn to frighten the animal out of her path. When the animal didn't budge, Dana slammed on her brakes and braced for an impact.

Scrambling for purchase on the asphalt, her back tires squealed and the tail end of the car whipped sideways. Dana clutched the steering wheel, turning into the skid and easing off the brakes. As the car straightened its course, Dana pumped the brakes until the car huffed to a stop, diagonal across the road.

She wheeled onto the shoulder, checked for her weapon and exited the car, clutching a flashlight. The smell of burning rubber and brake fluid assaulted her nose. The beam of her light played across the road in search of an injured animal. She hadn't felt an impact, but that didn't mean she hadn't grazed some poor creature.

The bushes at the side of the road rustled, and Dana spun around, her hand hovering over the gun in her shoulder holster.

"Who's there?" Remembering the night of the attack outside Auntie Mary's house, chills raced along her flesh. He'd moved silently that night, immobilizing her.

She yanked out her gun and trained it on the bushes. She'd be ready for him this time. He wasn't going to pull that voodoo crap on her tonight.

A soft breeze swirled through the air, caressing her skin. Her tense muscles relaxed as blackness engulfed her on all sides. She opened her mouth to protest this takeover of her senses, but the words remained lodged in her throat.

The bushes stirred again. Dana's gaze focused on a pair of golden orbs glowing in the night. Her gun dangled from limp fingers while the feral eyes mesmerized her.

A hollow voice echoed in her head. "Is this how he did it? Is this how he trapped his victims?"

A car engine roared in the distance, its headlights flooding the road. The animal disappeared and Dana sagged, her knees sinking to the ground.

The car screeched to a stop and footsteps clumped on the asphalt. Dana felt weightless as strong arms lifted her from the ground and Rafe cradled her against his chest. She clung to his neck, sobbing into his shoulder, his warmth breaking the spell.

"Are you all right? What happened?" His lips nestled against her hair. "Thank God I tried calling you."

After he'd settled her in the passenger seat of his squad car and bundled her in his jacket, he said, "What happened out there, Dana? Did you run out of gas? Did someone tinker with your car?"

"N-no. It was an animal."

His brows shot up. "An animal?"

She took a long pull from the bottle of water in his cup holder. "There was an animal in the road, and I swerved to avoid it. I wasn't sure if I hit it or not, so I got out to look for it."

At his exasperated sigh, she held up her hands. She wasn't going to allow him to berate her for not having her weapon handy this time. And this time she planned to tell him the truth.

"I had my gun out. When I heard rustling in the bushes, I pointed my weapon at the noise, but…"

"But what?" He'd grabbed her hand, which she hadn't even noticed had started trembling.

"Golden eyes." She cleared her throat. "There was a pair of golden eyes staring at me. They hypnotized me, Rafe, immobilized me. Th-the same thing happened that night outside Auntie Mary's place."

He swore and gripped her hand tighter. She stole a sideways glance at him and let out a pent-up breath. He didn't look incredulous or scornful. Lines of worry creased his face and furrowed his brow.

"Do you think this is our guy and he's using some kind of magical spell to lure his victims?"

A spiral of fear twisted in her gut. That's exactly what had occurred to her, and yet… "He didn't use a magical spell to lure Jacey. He used a very pragmatic text message."

"Maybe he's saving the mumbo jumbo stuff for you." Rafe squeezed his eyes shut. "Maybe he already knows about your gift, and he figures he has to fight fire with fire."

"I don't know, Rafe. It doesn't make any sense."

"I know who can make sense of it for us." He cranked on the engine.

Dana grabbed his forearm. "It's almost five o'clock in the morning. We can't wake Auntie Mary now."

He grimaced. "She's already awake. On my way back to the ranch, I called your cell. When you didn't answer, I called her house. She told me you weren't home. That's when I made a U-turn and came after you. I'm sure she's wide awake now."

"My purse and cell are still in my car. I'll drive back myself."

Rafe opened his mouth to protest and she landed a kiss on his scruffy chin. "You can follow right behind me. I promise I won't pull over for any animals. I'll just run right through them."

He snapped his mouth shut and grinned. "That's my girl."

When Dana returned to her car, she snapped on her seat belt and called her great-aunt, who scolded her for driving alone. But when she and Rafe arrived at her small house, shining like a beacon, Auntie Mary hugged her hard enough to crack bones.

"What happened? Not another attack?" Auntie Mary wrapped her shawl around narrow shoulders.

"Not exactly." Dana shot Rafe a glance and he nodded. "We want to ask you some questions about Southern Ute mysticism."

Auntie Mary quirked an eyebrow as she sank into her rocking chair by the fireplace. "You've come to the right place, but it's been a long time since you asked me about the old stories, Dana. Why now?"

As she settled on the carpet next to the rocking chair, Dana's cheeks warmed at the accusatory tone of Auntie Mary's voice. She hadn't shown any interest in the gift of the Redbird family since childhood. The time had come to put aside her pride. Lives depended on it.

"We think it might have something to do with these murders. The killer may be using magic or spells on his victims."

Auntie Mary closed her eyes and set her chair in motion. "Light the fire for me, Rafe. I have a chill in my old bones."

Rafe lifted his shoulders, and Dana jerked her thumb toward the fireplace and the wood stacked in the basket next to it. While Rafe lit the fire in the grate, Auntie Mary started to hum softly.

The tune struck a resonating chord in Dana's chest. She remembered Auntie Mary singing the Song of the Spirits to give thanks to the Ute spirits for the Redbird gift—the gift Dana had rejected. Until now.

Rafe sat next to her on the floor in front of Auntie Mary as the fire blazed to life behind them. Dana hooked her arm through his for support as they watched Auntie Mary's face, crisscrossed with lines of experience.

The humming stopped and Auntie Mary drew in a long breath that seemed to infuse her with energy and life. She began to speak, her voice strong and vibrant. "The great Sanawahv, the creator of Ute life and land, imbued certain animals with particular powers—birds, coyotes, bears and the most powerful of all, the wolf."

Dana gasped and the hair on the back of her neck vibrated. Rafe ran his hand along her back, warmed by the fire and further by the heat of his touch.

Auntie Mary opened her eyes and nodded. "Well, you should feel a connection to the wolf, Dana Redbird."

"I should?" Dana gulped as wisps of tales and legends floated through her mind.

"As shamans, the wolf is our protector, our guidance."

"Protector?" She pressed her palms to her temples. "I thought he wanted to devour me."

Auntie Mary stopped rocking and gripped the arms of her chair. "Now it's your turn to talk. Have you encountered a wolf spirit? How do you think the killer is using the Ute spirits? They wouldn't allow it, especially the wolf."

Rafe clasped Dana's hand while she told Auntie Mary about the attack outside her house where she heard the growl of an animal and saw his eyes. She also explained what happened earlier with the creature in the road and the golden orbs glowing in the bushes.

"So I figured the wolf had something to do with the killer, that somehow the killer was using the wolf to cast spells on these girls, to cast a spell on me." As she finished, Dana slumped against Rafe and he curled his arm around her shoulder.

Auntie Mary tapped her chin and stared into the fire. "The wolf is protecting you, Dana. He appeared when someone attacked you outside."

"But the attacker immobilized me. He had some kind of power over me."

"He might be attempting some kind of sorcery, which would anger the spirits, especially the wolf who protects the shamans."

"Why did the wolf appear tonight? Scared the stuffing out of me. That's not protection." She gave an exaggerated shiver, and Rafe pulled her even closer.

"Perhaps he's warning you." Auntie Mary lifted her shoulders. "Perhaps he wants something from you. Do you have something to offer?"

Dana dropped her chin to dodge her aunt's piercing gaze. "You know I don't use those powers, wouldn't know where to start."

Gripping her cane, Auntie Mary hauled herself from the rocking chair and Rafe jumped up to assist her.

"Now that the sun's up, I'm going back to bed for a few

hours." Auntie Mary shook off Rafe's hand. "Don't fear the wolf, Dana. Don't fear your powers."

When her aunt closed the bedroom door, Dana puffed out a sigh between pursed lips.

"Do you believe all that?" Rafe reached out and massaged her shoulders, easing the knots in her muscles.

"On an intellectual level? No. But on a gut-wrenching, been there done that, had the trance level? Yeah."

"So the wolf you thought you saw…" He raised his hands when she sputtered. "Sorry. The wolf you *saw* is protecting you."

"Don't stop." She rolled her shoulders, and Rafe resumed his massage with a grin. "Auntie Mary knows her stuff. If she says the wolf protects the Ute shamans, I believe it."

"What was he protecting you from on the road? Do you think the killer was following you or watching you? Maybe he was trying to protect you from me." He bared his teeth and growled.

Dana snorted. Nothing and nobody could protect her from Rafe McClintock. The way her brain turned to mush every time he touched her proved that. "I don't think the wolf was protecting me this time. I didn't feel the same terror I did during the attack—just that scary feeling from the mind control."

"Why did he appear?"

She scooped in a deep breath, the relaxation from Rafe's massage seeping away. "I think he was trying to communicate with me. When you drove up, you broke the spell, halted the trance."

"What do you think he wanted, a recommendation for a good rabbit stew?"

Dana knocked his hands away. "This isn't funny, Rafe. Why do you have to turn everything into a joke?"

"I'm sorry, sweetheart." He cupped her face in his large

hands and ran his thumb along the clenched line of her jaw. "I can see you're getting tense again and I wanted to diffuse the situation. Tell me what you think."

She dropped her lashes as her cheeks warmed. She'd always been too hard on Rafe. She hadn't had enough confidence in him. She'd dismissed him as a lightweight simply because he was always the life of the party, never understanding that his buoyant mood and party-boy image hid a wounded heart, a boy abandoned by his mother and desperate to hold on to the family he had left.

She knew she could trust the man before her now. She owed him that. And so much more.

"I didn't mean to snap at you." Her fingers traced the grooves of his knuckles. "I think this wolf spirit is telling me I have the power to unmask a killer. I felt it in the parking lot, Rafe. I told you Jacey called out to me, but it's not just Jacey. It's all the girls. They need justice."

"What do you plan to do about it?" He grabbed her hands.

"I'm going to give it to them."

"How?" His grip crushed her fingers, and his blue eyes burned with intensity.

"I'm going to pay Jacey Holloway a visit…in the morgue."

Chapter Eight

"No." Rafe yanked her toward him, placing her hands over his thundering heart. "I'm not going to allow you to put yourself in that kind of danger."

Dana's dark eyes sparkled, and she looked ready to bite his head off again. Then she uncurled her fists and laid her palm on his chest, her lips edging into a smile.

"I'll be fine. I'm a Ute shaman, remember? I'm protected by the wolf."

"I don't think any spirit can protect you from a serial killer—not once he finds out you're capable of identifying him." He trailed his fingers through her hair, its strands capturing the morning light as it streamed through the window. "You don't have to do this, Dana. We're going to check out Brice's cell phone today. We're onto something with that. We don't need your ESP."

"But it could help, and you know it. Don't tell me you hadn't hoped I'd seen something during the trance in Holly's room. I saw it in your face."

He opened his mouth, but she put her fingers on his lips. "I don't blame you, Rafe. If I can glean something, anything from a vision, it can only help. We both know it won't stand up in a court of law, but it just might lead us to a clue…or a person. The investigative work can take over from there."

"I don't want you to do this." He captured her hand and kissed each of her fingers. "I'm afraid of what you'll go through in one of those trances. I'm afraid of what you'll see. And I'm scared as hell the wrong person's going to find out you're playing with fire."

"Nobody is going to find out. We're not telling Emmett or Steve." She peered over his shoulder at the grandfather clock ticking in the corner. "What time is the autopsy today?"

"It's later in the afternoon, around three o'clock. Do you want me to pick you up?"

She smiled. "Seeing things my way?"

"Since you have the gift, I'll never quite see things your way, sweetheart. But I'll be damned if I'm going to let you have some creepy vision in a morgue with a dead body without me standing right by your side. When are you meeting Steve?"

"Nine o'clock and I'm exhausted."

He brushed the pad of his thumb along her cheek, edging the dark circle beneath her eye. "Get to bed and get a few hours of sleep before your meeting. I'm going to pick up Brice and head over to the Elk Ridge Bar. Rest up and eat a healthy lunch. I'll pick you up at two-thirty."

He tucked her hair behind her ears and kissed her mouth. "Just think of me as your wolf."

Two hours later, Rafe hitched a hip on the stool and smacked his palm on the smooth mahogany surface of the bar at the Elk Ridge Bar, Silverhill's most popular drinking establishment. "So who was in here last night, Chuck?"

Chuck Hernandez, proud owner of the Elk, screwed his eyes shut as he tilted his head back. "The usual suspects,

Sheriff. Hank, Greg, Scout. Even Joshua Trujillo was in here slumming it. Robert, Lenny, Theresa, Barb…"

As Chuck said each name, he ticked off a finger until he didn't have any left, and then he started over again. He opened one eye. "Your brother, Rod, was in here having a relaxing beer."

Rafe snorted. "I didn't know my brother relaxed. You said Lenny was in here? Lenny Driscoll?"

"Yep. He's been hitting the booze hard since he came back to town."

"Was he alone?"

"He was with Louella Thompson, Holly's mom. Damn shame about her girl and now Jacey Holloway. When are you boys going to stop this guy?"

"We're working on it." Rafe gulped down some tinny-tasting orange juice and grimaced. And if he could get some solid information from Brice and Chuck about what occurred at the Elk last night maybe Dana could skip her assignment at the morgue.

"I was sitting at the end of the bar." Brice pointed down the length of the bar. "Did you see anyone near my barstool or jacket when I was dancing?"

"You dance?" Rafe raised his brows.

A crimson flush raced up Brice's neck. "The ladies like to dance."

"From what I saw last night, I think you need to stop thinking about what the ladies like."

"You went home with Belinda?" Chuck smirked as he polished the same glass he'd been polishing since they walked in ten minutes before. "She's a man-eater, boy."

Brice blushed on top of his blush. "Can we get back to business here? Did you see anyone around my stuff?"

"Can't say that I noticed anyone. We had a full house last

night, dollar beer night, live band, hot mamacitas. You should come in more often, Sheriff. Hell, if that brother of yours can stop by, the former playboy of Silverhill can give it a try."

Rafe rolled his eyes at the title. No wonder Dana never took him seriously. "That was a long time ago, Chuck."

"Yeah, and you wouldn't have time now since Mary Redbird's great-niece is back in town. She's a fine-looking chica." Chuck shot Rafe a sideways glance.

Gossip whipped through Silverhill like a wildfire. That's what worried him about Dana's plan. "Dana's FBI. We have to work together."

"That's what they all say." Chuck winked at Brice. "Haven't seen much of Dana since she left for college. She's been back a few times, but mostly she flies Mary Redbird up to Denver. I think she's got a daughter or something."

"Dana doesn't have any kids." Rafe rubbed the back of his neck. At least he didn't think so. Did he even ask her about that?

Brice shook his head. "You're thinking of her cousin, Jennifer. She has a couple of kids and lives near Dana."

Rafe expelled a breath. Good. He didn't want to deal with any ex-husbands or ex-boyfriends—not when Dana seemed to be warming up to him.

Chuck finally put the glass away and picked up another. "Am I allowed to ask why you two are so interested in the Elk? Does it have something to do with Jacey's murder?"

"You're not allowed." Rafe slapped the bar. "Make me a list of everyone in here last night and ask your waitresses if they noticed anyone around Brice's stuff. We're going to have a look around."

While Chuck scribbled on a piece of paper, chewing on the end of a pencil between scribbles, Rafe and Brice canvassed the bar and the dance floor. No phone.

"This is all I can remember, Sheriff." Chuck waved the list in the air. "If I think of any more, I'll give you a call."

"Thanks, Chuck. You do that." Rafe plucked the piece of paper from Chuck's hand. He and Brice pushed out of the Elk and Rafe gulped in the clear, cool mountain air. The Elk smelled like cheap beer and stale cigarettes. Rod must've been desperate to stop in there last night.

"Okay, no luck there unless the waitresses remember something. Where did you park your car? Maybe you dropped the phone on your way out."

Brice scratched his unshaven chin. "I think the killer lifted my cell in the bar. He didn't just happen to find a cell phone in the parking lot and text Jacey. Somehow he knew I'd hooked up with her and knew she'd respond to a message from me."

"I knew there was a good reason why I hired you." Rafe punched his deputy's shoulder. "I think you're right, but Chuck was no help. If you were kicking it up on the dance floor all night, someone had plenty of opportunity to slip his hand in your jacket pocket and steal your phone."

Sawing his bottom lip with his teeth, Brice shoved his hands in his front pockets. "Do you think the killer already had Jacey picked out as his next victim? Was he biding his time, waiting for an opportunity to strike?"

"Maybe. But why did he select Jacey or any of them? With that text message, it doesn't look like these are random slayings. He's sending some kind of message. All the girls are full or half Ute."

Rafe's mouth went dry as he uttered the words that put a bull's eye on Dana's back. He settled his shoulders against his squad car and folded his arms, trying to block the uneasiness in his chest. "Were all the girls dating non-Native Americans?"

"Not Alicia. Her boyfriend was Patrick Rainwater, full-blooded Ute."

"That's right. Alicia always seems to be the odd girl out. All the others were into the party and club scene." Rafe swung his door open and slid onto the front seat. "I think we need to look at Alicia Clifton a little more closely."

"Are you going to the station?" Brice checked his watch. "Shift starts in less than an hour."

"I'll be there later. I'm going back to the ranch to get some breakfast, a little shut-eye and have a conversation with my brother about what he saw at the Elk last night."

When Rafe got to the McClintock ranch, he headed for the kitchen. Rod usually got up early to do some work on the ranch and then dropped by the kitchen for breakfast and to read the newspaper before heading out again.

Better him than me.

Rod, more than any of them, felt an attachment to the McClintock ranch. He wanted to preserve it. He wanted it to flourish. Maybe he remembered more of the good times when their mother still halfway acted like a mom.

Rafe's middle brother, Ryder, couldn't wait to get away from the place. He'd joined a covert ops group and had spent most of his twenties roaming around the world. When he discovered the love of his life living in Silverhill with their daughter, he finally settled down…but not in Silverhill.

Rafe couldn't wait to get away either, especially after Dana left for Georgetown. L.A. seemed like the perfect place to get lost, work a tough and dangerous job as an L.A. cop and blow off steam chasing skirts. The easy conquest of easy women soothed the dull ache in his heart, courtesy of a mom who didn't give a damn. That lifestyle had gotten old fast. He'd returned to Silverhill, yearning for something more substantial in his life, seeking roots. He'd felt that with Dana, and now fate had given them another chance…fate and a serial killer.

He went around to the side of the big house and stomped up the two steps to the kitchen door. He didn't want to catch anyone by surprise or in midargument.

Three smiling faces greeted him as his father, Pam and Rod all looked up from poring over drawings rolled out on the kitchen table. Rafe's eyes widened and he must've looked something like a fish since the smiles broadened into grins and then laughter.

"What are you staring at?" His father wiped his eyes and rested an arm across Pam's shoulders.

"Haven't seen the three of you enjoying each other's company much since I've been back." Rafe inched into the kitchen and poured himself a cup of coffee.

Ralph McClintock patted his wife's arm. "We've made a few decisions."

"Oh?" Rafe shifted his gaze from his father's worn face to his brother's inexpressive one.

"Tell him, Dad." Rod rolled up the plans and snapped a rubber band around them.

"Pam and I are leaving the ranch, leaving Colorado. Doc Parker's been after me to move to a warmer climate for years." He plowed stiff fingers through his thick silver hair.

"So you and Pam are happy to be going to, Palm Springs, is it? And Rod's just happy you're leaving?" Rafe slurped his coffee and scalded his tongue anyway. He'd returned to Silverhill to reconnect with family, and Ryder had wasted no time in spiriting away his new family and now Dad and Pam were leaving.

Ralph raised his shaggy brows. "You sound…irritated. I thought you were sick of the fighting?"

"I am." He tilted his chin toward the roll under Rod's arm. "And now maybe Rod will quit stomping around here growling since it looks like he's going ahead with plans for a dude ranch."

Rod smacked the roll against his hand. "Not so fast. We have a lot to work out first."

Dad frowned. "We're not leaving for a month or two. We heard about the Holloways' girl, Jacey. Hate to leave you in the middle of this nasty business."

"We plan on catching this guy a lot sooner than a month or two." Rafe rubbed his suddenly sweaty palms on the thighs of his jeans. And he hoped they could do it without endangering Dana's life.

"Hate to say it, but at least it brought that pretty little girl, Dana Croft, back to town. As I recall, you had quite a thing for her. Heard you've been spending a lot of time in her company." Ralph winked at Rod, who rolled his eyes.

"Yeah, well, that pretty little girl is an FBI agent now and we are investigating these murders. I've been spending a lot of time with her partner and Emmett too."

Ralph slapped him on the back, and Rafe nearly choked on his coffee. Hard to believe his larger-than-life father, his big frame only slightly stooped, had to move to a warmer climate for his health.

Her face pale, Pam gripped Ralph's arm and tugged. "We're going for a walk, boys. We'll be back in a few hours."

Rafe shrugged and splashed some milk in his coffee. "Do you want to show me those drawings?"

"They're sketchy right now, but don't worry. I don't have any intention of tearing down the guesthouse if you plan to stay there."

"I don't have any plans right now except to catch a killer."

Rod's eyes narrowed. "The old man's news seemed to shake you up. Don't tell me you're going to miss the old SOB, and I know you're not going to miss Pam."

"Hell, no." Rafe tossed his hat so that it hooked on the back of a chair. "I didn't realize the old man's health had deteriorated so much. That's all."

"Uh-huh." Rod leaned the heels of his hands on the counter behind him, hunching his shoulders. "'Cause you never struck me as the hearth and home type before."

Rafe snorted. "You got that right. Speaking of hearth and home or the lack thereof, I heard you were carousing at the Elk last night."

"I'd hardly call it carousing, but I did stop in for a few beers."

"Did you see my deputy Brice there?"

"Oh, yeah, and Belinda Mathers had her talons firmly planted in his backside. That boy had better watch himself. Belinda thinks her husband doesn't give a damn, but he's plenty fired up about her antics."

Rafe rubbed his hands. Good, he had caught his brother in a rare talkative mood. "Fired up enough to cause trouble for Brice?"

"Don't know, but Greg Mathers has been seething with fury for a long time."

Rafe mentally filed that piece of information away and felt in his pocket for Chuck's list of patrons. He pulled it out and handed it to Rod. "Did you notice any of these people around Brice or Belinda? Did you see anyone else at the bar who's not on this list?"

"What's this about?" He squinted at Chuck's cramped writing. "Are you asking me these questions in an official capacity?"

"Yeah, but I can't say any more than that. Somebody stole

something from the pocket of Brice's jacket at the Elk last night…and he wants it back."

Rod ran a thumb along his jaw as he studied the list. "Chuck has a better memory than I do. I don't recall half these people at the bar, and I left while Brice was still there. I do remember he was sitting at the end of the bar, near the front door. Anyone could've slipped in unnoticed and filched something from his jacket pocket."

Clenching his jaw, Rafe snatched the list back from his brother and smoothed it out on the kitchen table. Looked like he and Dana would have to keep that appointment at the morgue after all.

DANA FLEW DOWN THE STEPS of her aunt's house before Rafe could even kill the engine. A pair of gray slacks, high-heeled boots and a cobalt blue wool coat had replaced the worn denim jeans, furry boots and down jacket from last night. Dana had her professional armor firmly back in place.

From a distance, her appearance radiated confidence and swagger but when she slid into the patrol car next to him, her washed-out complexion and the dark circles bruising her eyes told a different story.

"You look tired. Are you sure you want to do this?" He brushed a lock of hair from her cheek.

"I have to do it. I couldn't fall asleep this morning. Those girls need my help. The Ute Tribe needs my help. I feel it here." She curled her hand into a fist and thumped her chest.

He clasped his hand over her fist. "Then I'll be there for you."

"You always were there for me, Rafe." She tilted her head and her eyes watered. "You would've supported me."

"Would have?" Her words didn't make sense. She must be tired. Rafe drew his brows together and smoothed the pad of his thumb across the back of her hand. "I'm supporting you now, sweetheart."

"I know." She closed her eyes and leaned against the headrest. "I suppose this means you didn't get anything out of Rod."

"He didn't have anyone to add to Chuck's list."

She sighed, keeping her eyes closed. "What did you tell the coroner about our visit today?"

"Correction. Silverhill doesn't have a coroner. Dr. Simpson, who has training in pathology, has been performing the autopsies on all the victims."

Opening one eye, she said, "I didn't realize Dr. Simpson wasn't a San Juan County coroner. Steve was okay with that?"

"Steve has the right idea—keep the investigation as local as possible. This isn't some big-city killer who's a stranger. This is a local man."

Dana hugged herself and shivered. "That's what makes this so creepy. So what story did you tell Dr. Simpson?"

"Didn't need a story." Rafe wheeled onto the highway back into town and the funeral home where Dr. Simpson would be performing the autopsy on Jacey Holloway later this afternoon. "I'm the sheriff of Silverhill."

TWENTY MINUTES LATER, they pulled into the empty parking lot of the Sharp and Heaton Funeral Home. Dana clasped her hands between her knees, staring straight ahead. *You can do this.*

Giving her a curious glance, Rafe got out of the car and came around to open the passenger door. "Are you ready?"

"As ready as I'll ever be." Dana swung her legs out of the car and straightened her back. As they walked up the stone pathway to the colonial-style building, Dana felt as if she were preparing for her own funeral.

They stepped into the hushed silence of the funeral home's lobby, and the heavy scent of lilies and furniture polish hung in the air. A lump formed in her throat as the smells brought back the memory of her mother's funeral.

Jerry Sharp, who ran the business with his brother-in-law, Frank Heaton, stepped out from behind the polished desk, his dark suit somber and appropriate.

"Afternoon, Sheriff. Dr. Simpson told me to expect you." Sharp adjusted his glasses before glancing behind him. "He hasn't done the autopsy yet, you know."

Rafe shook Mr. Sharp's pale hand. "We know that. There are a few things we want to check first. This is Agent Dana Croft. Dana, Jerry Sharp."

Sharp smiled as he took Dana's hand. "I feel like I know you since your aunt brags about you all the time. Are you going to stop him? We don't need this kind of business at our funeral home."

She ended the clutch of Sharp's cold fingers earlier than politeness dictated and cleared her throat. "We'll stop him. We're closer than ever. I can feel it."

Dana noticed Rafe's fists bunching his biceps as he watched Sharp's face. Rafe looked as jumpy as she felt. He couldn't keep running around assuming everyone knew about the gift or he'd unintentionally give her away.

Sharp nodded. "That's what we want to hear. Now if it's okay with you two, I'm going to join my partner at Mr. and Mrs. Holloway's place. We have a funeral to discuss."

Dana blew out a long steady breath. Good. They'd have the place to themselves. She didn't need anyone within hearing distance when she went into a trance. No telling what might happen.

Taking Dana's elbow, Rafe said, "No problem. If you could

direct us to the body and tell us how to lock up when we leave, we'll get started."

Sharp motioned for them to follow him down a small, dark hallway, the heels of his shiny black shoes clipping on the tile floor. He stopped in front of the last door on the left, pulled out a key ring and unlocked the door. "She's in here. When you leave, just pull the front door closed. It's already locked. I'll be back before Dr. Simpson arrives for the autopsy."

Mr. Sharp gathered a briefcase and cell phone from his desk. When the funeral director exited the building, Rafe pushed open the door and flicked on the light. The fluorescent glow emanated into the hallway, cast in shadows. The gray light chilled Dana's bones.

Rafe stepped into the room and extended his hand. "I'm right here for you, Dana."

She grasped his fingers like she was holding on to a lifeline and he gently pulled her into the room. Instead of leading her to life, he was leading her toward death.

Jacey's body lay on a table in the center of the gleaming white-and-chrome room, a white sheet covering her body. The fluorescent light emphasized her death pallor even more, contrasting sharply with her black, vibrant hair.

Dana hated this part of her job as an FBI agent. She swallowed and shuffled toward the table.

"Are you okay?" Rafe stroked her cheek, but even his touch couldn't warm her. She refused to let him see her fear. If he tried to talk her out of this, she'd cave in and run from this building like a rabbit from a wolf. Wolf. She had the wolf on her side, right?

She tossed her head and added a tough edge to her voice. "I've seen plenty of dead bodies, Rafe."

"Yeah, but not one that's going to talk to you."

Dana shrugged out of her coat and handed it to Rafe, who hung it on the hook on the door. Then she pulled off her gloves and stuffed them into her coat pockets. She turned to face the body again and set her jaw for Rafe's benefit and her own.

She was part of the Redbird family. It was time to acknowledge and embrace her heritage. Time to satisfy the expectations of the Ute spirit world and her ancestors. The power of her gift came from doing the right thing. The mission at hand had nothing to do with the circus sideshow acts Lenny forced her mother to perform.

Dana approached the examination table, rolling her shoulders and flexing her fingers like a concert pianist preparing for a performance. She tugged at the sheet, exposing Jacey's right arm. Jacey's red fingernail polish resembled drops of blood on the white sheet. One jagged nail marred the perfect manicure. Did she get that fighting off her killer?

Dana curled her fingers around Jacey's icy hand. When the warmth of her own skin connected with the deathly chill of Jacey's, an electric shock coursed through Dana's body. The current seemed to flow from her to Jacey, and the other woman's flesh vibrated in response.

Blackness edged Dana's peripheral vision and her head jerked back. She sensed movement from Rafe and heard a sharp intake of breath. If he touched her, she didn't feel it. She was slipping away from the physical world.

She moaned, a low guttural sound. Did that come from her or Jacey? She could no longer feel Jacey's hand. They had melded together. She didn't know where her body ended and Jacey's began.

Dana let go completely. Years of resistance and barriers melted away.

The vision took her.

Chapter Nine

She gagged.

Before he grabbed her throat, she'd felt warm, safe, secure…waiting for Brice. She squeezed her eyes shut, the smell of the latex gloves filling her nostrils. She clawed at his forearms, but her hands slid off the slick windbreaker jacket. She tried again, gathering the material in her fists this time, yanking to the sides. Her fingernail snapped.

Fear flooded her body with a rush of adrenaline. She kicked out, the point of her high heel meeting the solid leather of a cowboy boot. He kicked back, momentarily knocking her off her feet. He held her aloft with his hands around her throat and shook her like a rag doll.

She slumped, the energy from the adrenaline leaking out of her pores. Perhaps he was choking it out of her. As her strength waned, his seemed to grow. Like a monster feeding on her fear.

Her fingers wandered over the hands that clamped her neck in a vice. They stumbled across the heavy ring he wore on his left hand beneath the thin glove. As the fight seeped from her body, her lashes fluttered open.

A crown. A gold crown.

Dana choked and then coughed. A pair of strong hands encircled her waist…not her throat. Warm, safe, secure.

Her eyelids flew open and the harsh light of the examination room flooded her vision, hurting her eyes. She blinked and looked down at her hand, still clutching Jacey's cold fingers. Tears blurred her vision and she swayed, stumbling back.

Rafe wrapped his arms around her as he pulled her against his chest. Her head fell to the side, and a tear trailed into her ear where Rafe whispered assurances.

She couldn't bear the sight of Jacey's lifeless form so she turned in Rafe's embrace and buried her face in his shoulder. Pressing her nose against the rough material of his shirt, she inhaled his scent…clean, masculine, alive.

All of her losses rushed through her veins. She'd been a fool not to trust Rafe with her pregnancy. She'd allowed Pam to exploit her insecurities and play on her fears, never giving Rafe a chance to prove himself. Never giving him a chance to stand up to his father.

"Are you okay?" He cupped her face in his hands and ran a thumb across her cheek, catching a tear.

"I think so." She clasped his wrists lightly and locked her gaze on his eyes, drinking in their warmth, coming back to life. "Let's go back to the lobby and I'll tell you what I saw."

Rafe began to rearrange the sheet on Jacey's body and Dana grabbed his arm. "Wait."

She nudged the sheet from Jacey's legs and spotted an angry purple bruise across both shins. A kick from a cowboy boot. She yanked the sheet back into place.

Rafe grabbed Dana's coat from the hook on the back of the door and swung it open, gesturing for her to go through first. Dana took measured steps to keep from running out of the room.

The vision had scared the hell out of her. The murderer had

his hands around her throat just as surely as he had them around Jacey's. If Jacey had looked into the face of her killer before dying, Dana may have been able to identify him. As it was...

Rafe perched on the edge of Sharp's desk while Dana paced before the front window. She blew her nose, tossed the tissue in the trash can and then dug her heels in the floor in front of Rafe.

She told Rafe about her vision from start to finish. His face blanched beneath suntanned skin and he flinched a few times, but he let her finish.

"I didn't see the man's face, but I felt his hands and I locked on to Jacey's thoughts. We already know he wears latex gloves and I could smell those. He also wears cowboy boots, which doesn't narrow the field much, but now I know that indentation on the girls' throats is from a ring, a heavy ring on his left hand."

"Did you see the ring?"

"No." Dana's shoulders slumped. That part of the vision had disappointed her. She could smell, she could feel, she could taste the fear, she could even hear Jacey's choking and gasping, which had become her own, but she had remained in darkness. Was it because Jacey had her eyes squeezed shut?

Until the end.

A gold crown. Had she seen a gold crown? Imagined it?

"I—I might have seen a gold crown."

Rafe's brows shot up to the lock of hair curling over his forehead. "The killer was wearing a gold crown on his head?"

"On his head?" She hadn't thought of that. "I didn't actually see a gold crown I just flashed on the words. I was thinking a gold crown in his mouth, on his tooth."

"Chuck Hernandez, the owner of the Elk, has a gold tooth."

She drew in a quick breath. "Do you think he could've stolen Brice's phone and sent that message?"

"What? And then rushed over to the Shopco parking lot to strangle Jacey in the middle of a busy night at the bar? I doubt it."

"Maybe we have more than one guy out there. Maybe it's a team, you know, like the Hillside Stranglers."

"I think the likelihood of two serial killers discovering each other in a small town like Silverhill is remote. Maybe you saw or envisioned a gold crown like someone would wear on his head."

She chewed her bottom lip. "That's the problem. I didn't see anything. The words popped into my head. Do you really think someone is running around wearing a crown while he strangles women, like king for a day or something? Isn't that a little strange?"

"Because everything else about a man murdering women and then tying bandanas around their heads is normal?"

"You have a point." She plowed her fingers through her hair. "This isn't what I expected. I thought I'd just see the guy, we'd go to his house, find evidence and arrest him. Instead we're looking for someone who wears a gold crown and a ring on his left hand."

"You did great. Now we know he wears a ring."

"Yeah, like every other married man in town and on the reservation. That's not much help. Maybe I should…" Her gaze darted toward the hallway where Jacey rested in an uneasy peace.

"Negative. Dr. Simpson is going to be here to do the autopsy." He pulled her toward him and hooked his legs around hers. "Let's get out of here. How about some dinner later on, after you touch base with Steve and I go through Chuck's list with Brice?"

Dana placed her hands on Rafe's thighs, the strength of his solid muscles comforting beneath her palms. She needed comfort right now. She needed normal. She needed to escape the weight of the Redbird family legacy and its expectations, if just for one night.

"Dinner sounds great. It'll give me some time to think about what I saw. Maybe I'll have some better ideas when the fog clears a little more."

Rafe's lips skimmed her forehead. "Or maybe you're done thinking for today. You haven't been to La Paz since you've been back, have you? One margarita from La Paz and you'll be experiencing fogginess of another kind."

She nodded with a stupid grin plastered to her face. She'd never had a drink with Rafe before, never had a grown-up date with him. And when this investigation ended and they caught their man, she'd tell Rafe about Kelsey. Maybe he'd understand and forgive her.

Her cell phone rang and Dana extracted herself from Rafe and crossed the room to grab the phone from her purse. She peered at the display. "It's Steve. I'm late."

She answered the phone and told Steve she was on her way. Rafe had hopped off the desk and stood by the front door. "I'm going to get back to the station and touch base with Brice. We've been here a long time."

A key scraped in the lock and Mr. Sharp stepped through the door with Dr. Simpson close on his heels. "I was surprised to see your squad car still in the driveway, Sheriff. Did you get everything you needed?"

Dr. Simpson cleared his throat. "Is there a problem?"

"No problem." Rafe placed a steadying hand on the small of Dana's back. "We wanted another look at the mark on Jacey's neck. It's a bruise now, but it looks like it might be the band of a ring. Can you look at that more closely during the autopsy, Doc? Maybe take a few pictures?"

"Sure."

Dr. Simpson's gaze darted between her and Rafe and Dana's stomach flip-flopped. He didn't believe them. How could he possibly know what they'd been doing here? Maybe the ordeal of the vision still showed on her face.

She licked her lips. "No matter how many times I see a dead body, it always takes a toll on me. I'm looking forward to that drink at La Paz, Rafe."

He nodded. "I'll see you there at seven, after your meeting with Steve." He stuck out his hand. "Thanks, Mr. Sharp. How'd it go with the Holloways?"

Sharp lifted his black-suited shoulders. "How does it ever go? They're devastated."

Dr. Simpson clenched his jaw, one hand fisting at his side. "It's hard on the families, and then to add insult to injury the victims' lives are dissected and somehow they become the guilty parties."

"You know Alicia Clifton's family, don't you, Dr. Simpson?" Rafe squeezed the doctor's shoulder.

"This is killing them." Dr. Simpson wiped the back of his hand across his brow. "You have to stop this maniac before any more families are destroyed."

"We will, and your autopsies are going to help us. The FBI's been impressed by your work, Dr. Simpson. The fact that the Bureau hasn't called in its own pathologists speaks volumes about their respect for you. You'll help your friends, the Cliftons."

Dr. Simpson's red eyes watered as he nodded.

Rafe opened the door and Dana stepped outside, taking a deep breath. Maybe the FBI was wrong to rely on the locals. Everyone seemed to be taking this hard on a personal level.

She tucked a lock of hair behind her left ear. "Whoa. That

was intense. Did you get the impression Dr. Simpson was suspicious of us?"

"He was definitely jumpy." Rafe's blue eyes narrowed as he gazed at the jagged peaks of the Rockies. "Maybe we're reading too much into his behavior. It's gotta be tough doing an autopsy on an old friend's daughter."

"Is he friendly with the Holloways too?"

"Not like the Cliftons. He's skiing buddies with Jack Clifton, was best man at their wedding too."

Rafe continued to stare at the mountains, his thumbs hooked in his belt loops.

"What's wrong?"

"Alicia Clifton. It always comes back to Alicia Clifton."

RAFE CHECKED HIS WATCH. Ten minutes until he met Dana at La Paz. He saved the file on his computer that contained Brice's notes on the patrons at the Elk Ridge Bar. Dana's stepfather, Lenny Driscoll, had figured prominently in those notes.

One of the waitresses had remembered Lenny and his roaming hands. When she got off work early and left the bar, she recalled seeing Lenny in the parking lot with a cell phone in his hand and avoided him. Had he just sent Jacey Holloway a text message?

Rafe glanced at his watch again. Nine minutes. He blew out a breath and shoved back from his desk. Hell, it took a good five minutes to walk to La Paz, and Dana always arrived promptly. He didn't want to be late for their first real date.

He called out to his deputy who was yelling at a drunk in the jail cell. "I'm outta here."

It took him four minutes to walk to La Paz. He greeted the hostess and requested a table in the back. Even though he planned to steer the talk away from killers, dead bodies and visions, he and Dana didn't need anyone listening in on their conversation.

Ben Whitecotton, the curator of the new Ute Cultural Center, approached his table. "Evening, Rafe. Business or pleasure tonight?"

To give himself time, Rafe whipped the napkin off the table and dropped it on his lap. If he said *pleasure* and Ben saw Dana joining him, the gossipmongers would have a smorgasbord. If he said *business,* all ears would be trained toward their table. He took a sip of water. "A little of both. How's the cultural center coming along? We have security all lined up."

Ben flashed white teeth. "You read my mind. I was going to ask you about security. We're going to have some important artifacts on display, and we're expecting a big crowd."

"We have it all under control."

"Not quite, Sheriff." Ben shook back his long hair. "When are you going to stop this killer of our Ute women?"

Rafe steepled his fingers. Great. All they needed was for Ben Whitecotton to come after the police for racism. "It's the million-dollar question. What can I say? We're working on it. And you gotta know, Ben, we're investigating this just as hard as we would if the killer weren't targeting Ute women."

"I know that." He tilted his chin toward the door. "Because you have her on the case."

Dana sailed through the door of the restaurant, a furrow between her brows. She spotted Rafe in the corner and waved. Shrugging out of her coat, she approached the table. "Sorry I'm late."

"Two minutes. You're slipping, Agent Croft." Rafe stood up and pulled out the chair across from his.

A smiled tugged at her lips, but dark circles still bruised

her eyes and the frown hadn't left her face since she walked through the door. He'd have to fix that.

Placing her hand lightly on Ben's arm, she kissed his cheek. "Good to see you, Ben. Auntie Mary is really looking forward to the opening."

"She'll be one of my guests of honor. I hope we have a lot to celebrate by then." His gaze darted toward Rafe before he spun around and returned to his own table.

Dana hung her coat on the hook next to Rafe's hat and jacket and sank into the chair he'd pulled out for her. "What was that about?"

Rafe lifted his shoulders. He hadn't wanted to talk business, but it had already taken a seat at the table. "He was just implying we weren't working as hard as we could to catch this killer because he was targeting Native American women."

Her jaw dropped and she smacked the table. "That's B.S. Ben should know better. You practically lived at Auntie Mary's on the reservation our senior year in high school. Even though you were one of the high-and-mighty McClintocks, you treated everyone the same."

He spit a mouthful of water back in his glass. "The McClintocks were high-and-mighty? We were a mess."

"You know what I mean." She shoved her untouched glass of water toward him. "You were one of the four big ranching families along with the Pierces, the Scotts and…the Prices."

"Those families weren't all that high and mighty either, except maybe the Pierces. Ennis Price was eccentric and his son was a loser, and as I recall you and Tori Scott were pretty good friends. She never considered herself all that."

She smiled. "Yeah, well Tori was…Tori."

"She was a hell-raiser." Rafe waved the waitress over and ordered two margaritas. "The two of you couldn't have been more different."

By the time the margaritas arrived and Dana had taken her first sip, the vertical lines between her brows had smoothed out and her eyes had lost that hollow look.

Her long dark lashes lay on her cheeks as her tongue darted to the corner of her mouth to dislodge a grain of salt. "Mmm, this is good."

"Tell me about your life in Denver. You're not that far from Silverhill. How come you don't come back more often?"

"I'm busy." She swirled the pale yellow liquid in her glass and it sloshed over the rim. "My job is demanding. I ping-pong between Denver, D.C. and whatever Indian reservation the Bureau sends me to."

"Is that why you aren't married?" He traced a finger through the beaded moisture on the outside of his glass.

She took another swig of her drink. "Come on, I'm not even considered an old maid yet. There's plenty of time for all that."

"By all that, do you mean kids?"

"Hey, speaking of kids, I heard your brother Ryder has a little girl."

"Shelby, after our grandmother. She sure is cute. I never thought I'd be interested in having children, but a couple of hours with Shelby and I start thinking crazy thoughts."

"Are you ready to order?" Dana twisted her head to the side, looking for their waitress.

After an hour of conversation, spicy food and another round of margaritas, the knots in Rafe's neck had loosened. He and Dana had slipped back in time when the talk was easy and laughter bubbled around the edges. After those tense moments when he'd been stupid enough to mention marriage and children, Dana had relaxed and he took the opportunity to make her smile. He'd always been good at that.

Someone slapped Rafe on the back and he jumped.

"I knew it wouldn't be long before I found you two together." Joshua Trujillo showed a row of white teeth behind a phony smile.

Rafe shook Joshua's outstretched hand. "Hey, Joshua. How are your clubs doing?"

"Making money." He pulled up a chair to their table and straddled it. "I have to admit one club is doing better than the other."

Dana grimaced. "Let me guess. The topless one?"

"Bingo." Joshua made a gun with his fingers and pointed it at Dana.

Rafe rolled his eyes as he smirked at Dana. What did she ever see in this guy? Joshua had tried to bring gambling to the reservation, but the Southern Ute Council shot him down. Rafe approved of the decision. He didn't need that kind of trouble in Silverhill.

Dana batted his finger away. "Did Jacey Holloway ever frequent your clubs?"

Rafe raised his brows at the question. Dana obviously didn't see anything she liked in Joshua now. He and Emmett had questioned Joshua about his interview of Lindy for a job as a topless waitress at his club, but nothing came of that interview. Just another woman with low self-esteem looking to make a little money with her body, and just another businessman looking to exploit the situation.

"A few times." Joshua's Cheshire cat smile evaporated as he slid out of the chair and pushed it back under the table next to them. "All the victims showed up at my clubs, except for Alicia Clifton. That doesn't mean I killed them."

Dana tipped her head back to look at Joshua's flushed face. "So did Lindy take the job or not? 'Cause if she didn't, maybe that pissed you off."

Joshua backed away from the table. "I just came over to say hi, not to get interrogated. What happened to you, Dana? You used to be a fun girl in high school. Didn't she, Rafe?"

Joshua winked at Rafe before turning on his heel and sidling up to the bar.

"Yuck." Dana waved her hands in front of her face as if trying to disperse a noxious odor. "What happened to *him?* He's a creep."

Rafe lifted a shoulder as he pulled out some cash to pay the bill. "He started managing clubs and then opened his own. His position gave him access to a lot of women, and he liked the attention. Especially since he never got over the one who got away."

"Me?" Dana's voice squeaked as she pointed to herself.

"Every time I see him around, he brings it up—how I stole you from him in high school. He's joking, but there's something in his eyes…"

Dana shoved back her chair. "I thought we were just friends. Just goes to show you people aren't always what they seem."

"You got that right." As Rafe handed Dana her coat and grabbed his hat, trying to figure out a way to get Dana back to his guesthouse at the ranch, his cell phone buzzed in his shirt pocket.

"McClintock."

"Sheriff, this is Dr. Simpson. Sorry to interrupt your dinner, but I need to talk to you as soon as possible."

"We're just finishing up. Why don't you meet us here at La Paz?"

"I—I need to talk to you in private. I'm parked outside the McClintock ranch. I'll wait for you here."

"Is it the autopsy? Did you find something?"

"Meet me at the ranch."

Rafe slid his phone shut and raised his brows at Dana. "We might have a break here. Simpson's at the ranch."

"What are we waiting for?" Dana shrugged into her coat and beat Rafe to the door.

They discussed the possibilities of Dr. Simpson's findings on the way to the ranch, exhausting all the scenarios by the time they pulled up to the wide gate at the foot of the property.

Rafe waved to Simpson, and then hopped out of the car to swing open the gates. Simpson followed him down the side road that led to the guesthouse.

Rafe got out of his car and Simpson did the same, and then stopped in his tracks when he saw Dana.

"What's she doing here?" The finger Simpson pointed at Dana trembled.

"This is Agent Dana Croft. You met her this afternoon at the funeral home." Rafe reached out and pulled Dana to his side. Had doing the autopsies on local women finally gotten to Dr. Simpson? The man seemed unhinged.

Simpson snapped, "I know who she is. I asked to see you in private."

"We're investigating a serial killer, Dr. Simpson, and the FBI is involved. Anything you say to me, you can say to Agent Croft."

"All right, all right." Simpson's shoulders slumped and he shuffled toward Rafe's front porch.

Rafe exchanged a worried glance with Dana, and then bounded ahead of Simpson to unlock the door. He had left a lamp on, but flipped on the switch to the kitchen light. "Can I get you something? A drink?"

"Whiskey if you have it."

Rafe set up three short glasses on the counter that separated the small kitchen from the living room and took a bottle down from the cupboard. He splashed a couple of fingers of amber liquid in each glass and opened the fridge to look for something to mix with the whiskey.

"I'll take mine straight." Dr. Simpson held out a shaky hand for his drink and Rafe handed it to him. Simpson threw back the whiskey in one gulp and Rafe shoved another glass toward him. Simpson downed that one, too, and ran his palms along the sides of his wild hair, smoothing it into place.

"What did you find, Doc?" Rafe leaned his elbows on the counter and hunched forward.

"The Cliftons are my friends." Simpson removed his glasses and pinched the bridge of his nose. "I watched Alicia grow up. When she was murdered, I had already performed the autopsy on the first young woman. I knew it would be hard to do Alicia's autopsy, but I felt I was the man for the job and I wanted to help find her killer."

Dana joined Rafe in the kitchen and pressed up next to him, gripping the edge of the counter.

Simpson continued. "After I performed Alicia's autopsy, I went to my good friends first to tell them what I had found. I didn't want them learning the news any other way. What I told them broke their hearts."

Rafe slid his fingers along the counter and laid his hand over Dana's. "What did you find?"

"They begged me to keep it a secret. I knew it was wrong, but I couldn't refuse them. I was Jack Clifton's best man, for God's sake." Dr. Simpson wiped his eyes and Rafe ripped off a piece of paper towel from the roll and shoved it toward him.

Dr. Simpson blew his nose. "But then two other girls were

murdered. I've studied pathology. I know how important every piece of evidence is in trying to link murders of this sort. When I saw you two at the funeral home today, I thought maybe you'd discovered my cover-up. Then it didn't matter whether or not you'd discovered it. I couldn't keep it a secret anymore. Not after Jacey's murder. I swear that girl on the slab today pleaded with me to reveal the truth and find justice for her and Alicia."

Rafe held his breath while Dana whispered, "What truth, Dr. Simpson? What did you discover during Alicia's autopsy?"

Simpson balled the paper towel in his fist and replaced his glasses.

"Alicia Clifton was pregnant."

Dana sagged against him, and Rafe hooked an arm around her shoulders. Alicia Clifton wasn't so different from the other victims after all. At least a deranged killer might see it that way.

"How far along was she?" Dana asked.

"About seven weeks." Dr. Simpson ran a hand over his haggard face. "I'm sorry I didn't put this information in the autopsy report. I was just trying to spare some friends further agony."

A muscle twitched in Rafe's jaw. He could understand trying to protect friends but not at the expense of a serial murder investigation. "Do we know who the father was? Alicia was buried weeks ago. I suppose there's no chance of collecting DNA now. What if the killer was the baby's father?"

"No." Dr. Simpson held up his hand. "The father was definitely Patrick Rainwater, Alicia's boyfriend. Alicia wouldn't sleep around."

"Had she told Patrick about the pregnancy?" Dana's voice sounded strained, the casual laughter at dinner completely wiped away.

Dr. Simpson toyed with the third glass of whiskey and then pushed it away. "We don't know."

"You don't know?" Rafe slammed his fist on the counter. "You didn't bother to ask Alicia's boyfriend, the probable father of her baby if he knew about the pregnancy? God, what a mess. This is what lies get you. We've lost precious time here, Simpson."

"I'm telling you now. Go question the boy. I have to break the news to the Cliftons that their secret is out." He wiped his hand across his mouth and stumbled toward the front door.

"And with that secret revealed, we have a better chance of catching Alicia's killer." Rafe followed Dr. Simpson and slammed the door after him.

"Damn."

The glasses clinked as Dana rinsed them out and placed them in the sink. She turned to face Rafe, her hands behind her clutching the counter, her complexion pale. "We have to report Dr. Simpson to the Medical Examiners Board."

"I suppose so." Dropping to the sofa he clutched his hair. He hated this part of being the local sheriff for a small town. He didn't want to upset any residents of Silverhill, but he and Dana would have to share this new information with Steve and Emmett. And Steve was no local.

The sofa cushion sank as Dana settled beside him. "You don't think Alicia's boyfriend had anything to do with her murder, do you?"

"I don't think so, but Alicia's murder bothered me all along. Think about it. All the other girls were into partying. I'm not judging them, but they had reputations for sleeping around. But not Alicia. This pregnancy may tell another story about her. Maybe she cheated on Patrick. Maybe the killer's connection to all these young women is that he slept with them."

Dana leaned forward, planting her elbows on her knees. "Looks like we need to talk to Patrick again tomorrow."

"I agree. Do you want to come with me?"

"Sure, but I'd better get going. It's been a long day. Can you drop me off at my car?"

She pushed up from the sofa and he grabbed her hand. He didn't want her to leave. He'd been trying to figure out how to get her back to his place when Dr. Simpson's call solved the problem for him. Just his luck the call had also spoiled the mood.

"It's late. I don't want you driving back to the reservation from town. Remember what happened last time?"

"Now that I know the wolf is my friend, I'll be fine." She grinned but left her hand in his.

"You shouldn't be driving." He ran the pad of his thumb beneath her eye. "You look exhausted."

She slapped his hand and he jumped back. "I thought you were supposed to be smooth with the ladies, McClintock. Here you are trying to seduce me by telling me I look like a washed-out hag."

He exhaled a long breath, releasing a knot in his chest. "Believe me, sweetheart, if you're a hag I don't know the meaning of the word. And how do you know I'm attempting a seduction?"

"You have me in your lair, and you want to keep me here."

"You don't believe I'm concerned about your safety?" He wrapped an arm around her waist and drew her close, snugly fitting her to his body.

"Oh, I know you are." Her smooth hand caressed his cheek. "But you have ulterior motive written all over your—" she glanced down at his crotch pressed against her hip "—face."

He chuckled. "So concern for your safety isn't seductive?" He turned his head and kissed her palm, satisfied by the little ripple that flowed through her body.

"No."

"So what is…seductive, I mean?"

"Hmm." She raised her eyes to the ceiling. "I like to have my hair stroked."

"Like this?" He weaved his fingers through her silky strands, skimming through the length of her dark hair.

Sighing, she closed her eyes. "Yesss."

"What else?"

"I like a nice back massage."

"Like this?" His hands inched down until he kneaded his fingers into the tight muscles between her shoulder blades.

A small moan escaped her lips while her head dropped to the side. His fingers trailed along her spine and he rubbed the small of her back. Tucking his fingers into her back pockets, he pulled her up against his body.

"What next?"

Her lashes fluttered as her lips parted, but she seemed incapable of uttering a coherent word. Her instructions for seduction had worked perfectly.

Tracing the outline of her mouth with his fingertip, he brushed his lips against hers. A flame ignited in his belly, but he squeezed his eyes shut and clenched his jaw. Dana wanted a seduction, not a conquest.

"Don't stop." She rasped her knuckles across the stubble on his chin. "You were doing just fine."

Threading her fingers through his hair, she pulled his head back down to hers and captured his lips in a kiss so sweet and so hot, he tasted burnt sugar. His tongue toyed with hers and then he deepened the kiss.

It was like high school déjà vu—the impatience, the sensory overload…the nerves. Damn. He hated to admit it, but the prospect of making love to Dana had ratcheted up his anxiety level. She'd expect so much more out of him now, wouldn't she?

He pulled out of the kiss and placed two fingers over her protesting mouth. "I have a room now and a bed. No more caves."

She puckered her lips and sucked his fingers into her mouth, and then playfully bit them. "Too bad. I kinda liked the cave."

To hell with seduction. He scooped her up in his arms and charged toward the bedroom. Tonight he'd make her forget. Forget the cave. Forget why she ran. Forget the murders. Forget the visions.

He dropped her on the bed, thankful he'd remembered to make it this morning, and pulled at the buttons on his shirt.

"Whoa, cowboy." She rose to her knees, hooked her fingers in his waistband and pulled him forward. "Let me do the honors."

He felt like jumping out of his skin. Every time she undid a button on his khaki shirt, her nails trailed along the T-shirt beneath. When the shirt gaped open on his body, she peeled it from his shoulders, letting it drop on the floor. Then she tugged at his T-shirt, still tucked into his jeans, and skimmed her hands along his torso as she pulled it up.

He raised his arms so she could take it off, but she stopped, leaving the T-shirt hooked around his shoulders and covering his head. Her lips touched his midsection, feeling like a hot brand. She laid a path of kisses up to his chest, and then worked downward until she reached the belt on his jeans. Her tongue flicked along his belly above his waistband and he ripped the T-shirt from his head and grabbed her shoulders to steady himself.

Where had she learned these exquisite torture techniques?

She unbuckled his belt and unzipped his fly. As she reached to pull down his jeans, he grabbed her hands.

"Those aren't going anywhere until these do." He pointed to the silver tips of his boots. He sat on the bed next to her, crossed an ankle of his leg and tugged at his right boot.

She settled on the floor in front of him, still fully clothed. He'd have to remedy that…fast. He pulled off his boot and extended his left leg toward her. She tugged off his other boot and slipped off both of his socks.

"Now that all those impediments are out of the way, let's get to the main attraction."

He choked on his fake indignation as he stood up. "You've gotten brazen in your old age, Croft."

And it turned him on.

While she slid his jeans down, her hands skimmed his thighs. Before he even kicked them off his legs, she went for his boxers and yanked those down too. She brushed her fingernails along his length, and he shivered from the sheer effort of refraining from taking her in his arms and devouring her.

"You've gotten…better in your old age, McClintock."

He'd show her how much better. Without touching any other part of her body, he kissed her until she became breathless and placed her palms against his bare chest to recover.

"You must've had a lot of experience to learn to kiss like that. While I'm sure my experience is modest compared to yours, I've learned a few tricks myself." Her gaze locked on his and her hands began roaming over his body—skimming, pressing, tweaking, kneading.

He couldn't take another second. Capturing her hands, he growled, "Are you finished toying with me?"

Her eyes widened as she dipped her chin. She kicked off

her heels and shrugged out of her suit jacket, and they both scrambled to relieve her of the rest of her clothing.

Rafe grinned. *So much for the slow seduction.*

They fell to the bed together, clasped in an embrace. His body pressed along the curvy lines of hers, still Rafe felt he had to get closer. His fingers tangled in her hair and his lips traced every ridge and hollow of her chin, her neck, the base of her throat. He shaped her breast and circled the nipple with his tongue. Sighing, she arched her back and dug her nails into his scalp.

"Does that mean you want me to continue?"

She playfully smacked the top of his head. "If you quit now, I'll have to jump into the Silverhill Creek stark naked to cool down."

"I could probably sell tickets to that."

She shoved his head back between her breasts, and he continued his journey down her café au lait skin. When he reached the juncture of her legs, he ran his tongue along her musky sweetness. The breath hissed between her teeth as she clutched the bedspread in white-knuckled fists.

Reaching her climax, she called out his name over and over and it had never sounded sweeter.

He didn't want to delay their ultimate connection any longer. He entered her hard and fast while she still thrashed in the throes of her passion. She clawed at his buttocks, urging him on, whispering her need of him in his ear.

When he exploded inside her, he quenched a yearning that had lasted for ten long years. As he rode out the last wave of his climax, he kissed her, long and completely…and possessively.

He rolled onto his side and pulled her back against his chest, resting his chin on her shoulder. He hooked a leg over her hip, not ready to give up what he'd just reclaimed.

"This is the safest I've felt since returning to Silverhill." She ran her fingertip along his thigh. "You always made me feel safe."

"If you always felt safe with me, why'd you leave?"

Then the bedroom window exploded in a crash.

Chapter Ten

Rafe crushed Dana against him for a moment before leaping from the bed. A jagged hole gaped in the window and shattered glass littered the hardwood floor. A large rock lay amid the debris.

"What is it?" Dana sat up, clutching the sheet to her chest.

"Someone lobbed a rock through the window." Rafe crouched at the boundary of the glass and squinted at the rock, which had landed beyond the glow of light from the lamp on the bedside table. He shoved to his feet, pulled on his boxers and grabbed one of his discarded socks.

"Don't worry." He patted Dana's back, but she was already scrambling for her clothes. "It's probably some moronic kid."

With his hand shoved in the sock, he leaned forward and picked up the rock. Dana's sharp gasp at his shoulder told him she'd already seen the words crudely printed on the rock.

Each victim's name and in the last spot…a question mark.

Dana's stomach clenched while she dug her fingernails into Rafe's shoulder. The killer had been out there with a message for Rafe—a message for her?

Rafe dropped the rock on the bed and dove for his clothes. "I'm going after him."

A bright light flooded the room and an alarm started a rhythmic buzzing. Dana grabbed her blouse, plunging her arms in the sleeves. "What's that?"

"The guy must've tripped the security system on his way out. We had it installed after Ryder's little girl was kidnapped from the ranch." Rafe stuffed his feet inside some running shoes and charged into the living room.

Avoiding the glass on the floor, Dana followed him. "I'm coming with you."

"If he triggered the alarm, he's either at the big house, which I doubt, or he slipped past the perimeter of the property." He plucked his gun from the holster hanging over a kitchen chair.

Dana grabbed her own weapon and, cursing her high heels, ran onto the porch after him. "Which direction?"

A figure emerged from the shadows of the guesthouse and Dana spun around, leveling her gun at the intruder.

"What the hell is going on?" Rod, a pair of flannel pajama bottoms hanging low on his hips, his hair sticking up in all directions, emerged with his hands in front of him.

Rafe jerked his head back. "Someone tossed a rock through my bedroom window."

"And that warrants full firepower?"

"The rock had all the murder victims' names on it."

Rod cursed and then cupped his hands over his mouth and shouted into the darkness, "We need some help here."

A couple of men in various stages of undress, Dana assumed ranch hands, jogged forward. Rafe strode off the porch shouting orders.

"You're coming with me." He grabbed her arm, pulling her with him toward the back of the guesthouse.

"Wait." She dug her heels into the dirt. "Nobody's checking across the paddock toward the riding trail."

Rafe's grip tightened. "I want you with me."

"I'm an FBI agent with a weapon. Let me do my job." She twisted out of his grasp and stepped back.

He matched her a step forward, but then clenched his jaw and brushed her cheek with the back of his hand. "Be careful."

"You too." She unhitched the gate and picked her way across the riding paddock, her heels scraping against the packed earth. The beam from the flashlight Rafe had pressed into her hand traced footprints in the dirt, too numerous to have any significance.

She froze when she heard leaves crunching at the edge of the paddock, and then she swung her flashlight toward the noise. She crept forward, her gun and flashlight leading the way.

She peered between the slats of the gate that led to the riding trail beyond and flicked the padlock with her gun. The beam from her flashlight glinted over the barbed wire encircling the top of the gate and the fence. No way the intruder could've come from this direction. Nothing cut, breached or compromised.

Clinging to the gate, she squinted at the first bend in the trail, the darkness just beyond the reach of her flashlight. Twigs snapped and the hair on the back of her neck quivered.

"Hello?"

Ridiculous. Would a wild animal respond? Would the killer?

Something watched her from beyond. Her eyes ached as she scanned the blackness of the trail. Was it her protector again? The wolf?

How did she even know the wolf was on her side? Hadn't Auntie Mary's legends contained stories about evil forces compromising the shaman's familiars?

Great time to remember that.

Keeping her gaze—and gun—pinned to the shadows obscuring the riding trail, Dana backed up one step at a time. She bumped into a solid form behind her. She spun around, screaming and swinging her gun in front of her.

"Hey!" Rafe knocked her wrist up so that her gun pointed skyward. "What are you doing, Dana? I called you three times as I came across the paddock. I thought you heard me."

Dana gulped a second scream and planted her feet on the ground to prevent herself from flinging herself into Rafe's arms. She'd better snap out of these trances or Rafe would begin to question her sanity, or at least her competency to carry a loaded firearm.

"I thought I heard something out there." She pointed her weapon toward the trail beyond the paddock.

"Let's check it out." Rafe pulled a large key chain from his belt loop and asked her to shine her flashlight on it while he searched for a key.

After a few tries, one of the small keys he selected clicked open the lock on the gate and he pushed it open.

Dana nestled close to Rafe's back as he stepped onto the riding path. His flashlight created an arc of yellow, highlighting the ground before them. She held her breath as they approached the turn in the trail. They rounded the corner and the path stretched into darkness once again.

Dana crouched on the ground and ran her hand along the leaves of a bush, its narrow branches snapped here and there. "What do you think of this?"

Rafe knelt beside her, fingering the broken twigs. "I don't see any clear footprints. Could be an animal."

That's what concerned her. Standing up, Dana brushed her hands on her slacks. "Did anyone else find anything?"

"Not that I know of. You were one of the last to return. You had me worried."

"Probably took me longer since I don't know the property like you and the rest."

By the time Dana and Rafe arrived at the big house, lights blazed from every window and a knot of people were crowded on the porch.

She swallowed hard when she saw Pam, wrapped in a housecoat, clutching her husband's arm. Dana squared her shoulders. *Don't be ridiculous. You're not an insecure teenager anymore…and you've got a gun.*

When they reached the circle of light, Rafe hooked his arm around her shoulders and pulled her in close. "I found her. She heard something outside the paddock, but we didn't see anything."

"Did anyone else find anything suspicious?" She squirmed out of Rafe's embrace. Bad enough that Rod had caught her at the guesthouse after hours, now Rafe was hugging her in front of the entire family. She dragged in a deep breath and had to remind herself again that those high school days were long gone.

Rod and the few ranch hands who'd been searching the property hadn't found any evidence of a break-in or a breach in security.

No trace of an intruder at the ranch. No witnesses to the theft of Brice's cell phone. No evidence on the bodies. Were they trying to capture a man or a phantom?

Dana shivered and hugged herself.

Rafe ran a hand down her back and then captured her hand, dragging her closer to the assembly in front of the house. "Dad, Pam, you remember Dana Croft, don't you?"

Rafe's father, Ralph, leaned forward and grabbed her other hand and squeezed. "Sure do. How's Auntie Mary? I don't see nearly enough of her around town."

"She's doing great." She glanced at Pam. "How are you, Pam?"

Pam inched out a tight smile as her gaze raked over Dana, most likely noting her disheveled appearance. "Busy taking care of my family. I understand you're a highly regarded FBI agent. Congratulations on your success. You seem to have made the right choices in life."

Dana clenched her teeth. Keeping Rafe from his daughter had *not* been the right choice. She knew that now more than ever. "Oh, I don't know about that. I've made my share of mistakes, but I plan to remedy some of those."

"You're lucky." Pam huddled next to her husband. "Most of us can't fix the mistakes we've made. We just learn from them and move on."

"Sometimes you can't move on until you correct a past folly."

With a crease lining his forehead, Rafe had been shifting his gaze back and forth between her and his stepmother. "Does anyone here care that a serial killer sneaked onto the ranch and threw a rock through my window?"

Pam broke eye contact first, and a buzz of victory fizzed through Dana's veins. She had Pam on edge. She had the upper hand because she had truth on her side…or she would once she told Rafe about Kelsey.

"I do." Rod smacked the railing on the porch. "I paid a lot of money for that security system, and some nut job just strolls onto the ranch and tosses rocks at your window?"

"How do you know it's really the killer and not some irate

Silverhill citizen who's angry because you can't catch this guy? When *are* you going to do your job and catch this guy?" Ralph draped an arm around his wife's trembling shoulders.

Dana couldn't figure out if Pam's fear sprang from the break-in at the ranch or Dana's reappearance in Rafe's life bearing ten-year-old secrets.

"Unbelievable." Rafe dragged a hand through his tangled hair. "Rod's worried about his precious ranch, and you can't waste an opportunity to get a dig in about the job I'm doing."

"Just do that job, boy, and we'll all be a lot safer." Ralph tucked an arm around Pam and led her back into the house.

Rod lifted his shoulders and followed them inside, slamming the door behind him. The locks clicked into place, but Rod left on all the lights lining the front drive along with the ones lighting the path to the guesthouse.

Rafe turned his back on the house, shoving his hands in his pockets and hunching his shoulders. "That's my loving family for you."

"M-maybe you should take me back to my car in town." Dana jerked her thumb over her shoulder.

"I'm not up for a drive, and I sure as hell don't want you heading back to the reservation." He grinned. "It's too late now, anyway. I'm sure my family already figured out we weren't poring over case files when the rock sailed through the window."

"Maybe we should pore over case files. There's no way I'm going to fall asleep tonight."

"I'm going to bag that rock as evidence and get it dusted for prints tomorrow. In the meantime, I have a better plan than sleep." He laced his fingers through hers and tugged her toward the path leading to the guesthouse.

Resting her head on his shoulder, Dana sighed. She'd been on a roller coaster of emotions today, but sharing a meal…and a bed with Rafe had eased the stresses of the day and had even made them bearable.

Now she just wanted back in his arms where she belonged because once he found out about Kelsey, he might never offer again.

"I'M NOT GOING TO LIE TO YOU, Rafe. This meeting in Denver is about sending a full FBI task force down here if we don't make progress soon." Steve scratched his chin as Rafe, Emmett and Dana all stared at the rock in the center of the conference table, willing it to give them more information than the victims' crudely printed names.

Dana slanted a gaze toward Rafe and his tight jaw. First his father had accused him of incompetence and now the FBI planned to swoop in and take over the case. He'd hate that. As the youngest McClintock brother, Rafe had always been the charmer, the lightweight of the family. But Dana knew he'd worked hard to dispel that image. The people of Silverhill trusted him as their sheriff. If he failed now, would he lose that hard-earned trust?

"We still need to talk to Patrick Rainwater." She rolled the disappointing rock back into its evidence bag. No fingerprints. Crude block letters written with a common felt-tip pen. No evidence left at the ranch. Nothing. "The fact that Alicia was pregnant changes a few pieces of this puzzle."

"Can you and Rafe take care of that?" Emmett wagged his finger between the two of them. "I know his parents too well. He'd never open up with me there."

Dana bit her lip. Steve didn't need to hear that piece of information either—more ammunition for bringing in the task force. "We'll handle Patrick. What time is your flight, Steve? Can we give you a lift to the airport?"

Steve checked his watch. "My flight's soon, and yeah, I need a ride."

After Dana and Rafe drove Steve to the airport in Durango, they headed for the reservation to talk to Patrick. He lived with his parents while he commuted to Fort Lewis College in Durango, but they'd called ahead to make sure they could meet him this afternoon. Dana figured he'd be glad his parents were at work.

They pulled up to the neat stucco house, and Patrick emerged onto the porch to intercept them, his eyes worried behind glasses. "My mom's home from work. Can we talk out here?"

Patrick led them to the corner of the yard, edged with a garden of flowers and two wrought-iron benches, and safely out of his mother's earshot.

Dana settled on the uncomfortable bench and pointed across the street at the rust-colored adobe building. "Are you going to mind being so close to the cultural center when it opens?"

"Huh?" Patrick had removed his glasses and was wiping them with his shirt. "The cultural center? No, I don't mind it so close. I helped Ben with the layout of some of the items. I'm doing my minor in Native American studies at Fort Lewis."

"Why don't you have a seat, Patrick?" Dana patted the bench beside her as Rafe tipped his hat over his eyes.

Patrick licked his lips, his eyes flicking to Rafe. "I'm good where I am."

"Patrick, did you know Alicia was pregnant?"

He dropped to the bench, clutching his head in his hands. As his shoulders shook, Dana sucked in her bottom lip and laid a hand on his back. "I'm sorry, Patrick."

He raised his head, his eyes red and his nose running. "How did you find out? I was wondering why that never came out after her…death. I figured, you know, I mean, I thought that they'd discover that during her autopsy."

Crossing his arms, Rafe wedged a shoulder against the tree trunk. "The doctor did discover that during the autopsy, but he covered it up because he's good friends with the Cliftons. Why didn't you tell someone? I questioned you about your relationship with Alicia after her murder. You didn't think it was important to mention that little detail?"

Patrick jumped up and ran his shirtsleeve beneath his nose. "I don't know. I didn't think it would matter. I didn't want Alicia's parents to find out."

"Do you know for sure the baby was yours?" Rafe pushed off the tree and stood blocking Patrick's path.

Patrick's mouth dropped open. Then he balled his fists and took a step toward Rafe, who squared his shoulders and widened his stance.

"Of course it was mine. Alicia was a virgin. We both were, and we were planning to get married. I don't have to listen to this B.S."

Patrick spun back toward the house, and Rafe grabbed his arm. "Son, this is a murder investigation. You do have to listen to this B.S. Did anyone else know about the pregnancy?"

Patrick glanced at Rafe's hand before shaking it off. "No. We kept it a secret. Now you know. I lost my girlfriend and our baby, and my grief is my own business."

Rafe's eyes narrowed as he watched Patrick stomp back to his parents' house. "Do you believe him, or do you think he kept Alicia's pregnancy a secret to hide a motive for murder?"

Dana rose from the bench, dusting the seat of her slacks. "I don't think pregnancy is much of a motive."

"Unless the baby belonged to someone else and Patrick found out about it."

"But how would that connect him to the other women?"

"Maybe they were all fooling around with the same guy." Rafe pinched the bridge of his nose, screwing his eyes shut. "We just haven't run across any boyfriends in common yet, except my deputy, but that doesn't mean we won't. Anyway, I have some work to do at the station. Do you want a ride back into town or to Auntie Mary's?"

Dana folded her arms and gazed at the peaks of the Rockies in the distance. She and Rafe hadn't discussed the night they'd shared together yet. They had made love and slept in each other's arms. They had laughed and whispered and soothed each other's worries. Their connection smacked of together forever. But before they could get started on forever, she had a huge secret to reveal. And Rafe had to forgive her.

Right now that hurdle seemed as high as those peaks.

Her gaze dropped to the adobe cultural center, a seamless addition to the Colorado landscape. "You can leave me here. I'm going to peek in at the cultural center. I can walk back to Auntie Mary's or Ben can give me a lift. Are you going to the opening of the cultural center?"

"I wouldn't miss it."

Rafe kissed her lightly on the lips and waved out his car window as he drove away.

She wandered across the street, chewing her bottom lip. She had a decision to make. What if they never solved this case on their own? What if Steve's meeting today resulted in the FBI forming a task force down here? They'd pretty much take Emmett and Rafe off the case then. Could she add insult to injury at that point and tell Rafe about the daughter she'd kept from him all these years?

She stumbled up the wide steps of the cultural center and pushed open the unlocked door. "Hello? Ben?"

Ben emerged from his office, slicking back his ponytail, his face flushed. "Hello. What can I do for you?"

Dana tilted her head at his formal tone, then stepped back when Ben's office door swung open behind him.

"Hi, Dana. Whaddya think of the place?" Her stepfather, Lenny, barreled into the room.

What was he doing here? The only interest Lenny had in Ute culture was bleeding it dry for financial gain. "This is a surprise. I had no idea you were an aficionado of Southern Ute culture."

"Don't quite get the meaning of your fancy Georgetown word, but why should you be surprised to see me at the cultural center? I've lived among the Ute for many years, married one and just might marry another."

"You and Louella Thompson are getting married?" She gripped the strap of her purse.

"We're thinking about it." The corner of his mouth lifted in a half grin.

Ben cleared his throat. He had been shuffling papers behind the desk at the entryway during their conversation, his color still high.

Dana jerked her head back toward Lenny. "What were you doing in Ben's office?"

Lenny's grin stretched across his teeth. "Why, I believe I'd classify that information as none of your business, baby girl."

She dug her fingernails into her upper arms. She hated Lenny's old nickname for her. Unfortunately, she didn't have any right to know the details of his conversation with Ben. Conversation or argument?

Her gaze darted toward Ben, but he'd retreated behind the lobby desk, lips pursed. Obviously, she'd get nothing from him. Ben wasn't easily agitated, but he sure didn't look happy coming out of that office.

Her cell phone buzzed in her pocket and she excused herself and turned her back on the two men. She sucked in a breath when she saw the display—Kelsey. Was she out of school early today?

"Hey, you."

Her daughter's voice, high and breathless, answered. "Hi, Mom. Are you okay?"

"Of course." Dana wrinkled her nose. "What's the matter?"

"N-nothing. I'm all right."

Dana's heart pounded as she checked her watch again. Kelsey should definitely still be in school. Aware of the silence of the two men behind her, she strolled to the window and lowered her voice. "Why aren't you in school? I know they don't let you turn on your cell phones during school hours."

"I'm not in school."

A spiral of fear coiled up Dana's spine. "Where are you, Kelsey? Are you in trouble?"

"No, I'm not in trouble, Mom, but I'm afraid you are."

Chapter Eleven

Dana clutched her little cell phone so tightly, its edges bit into her fingers. "What do you mean? I'm fine. Where are you?"

"I'm at the Durango bus depot."

Dana threw out an arm and grabbed the windowsill. "What are you doing here?"

"Are you all right, Dana?" Ben had come out from behind the desk, his brows drawn over his nose.

"I'm fine," she lied. "I have to take this call outside. FBI business."

Ignoring Lenny's lazy stare, she strode toward the double doors of the cultural center and then tripped down the steps. Her firm voice compensated for her trembling knees. "Okay, young lady. Explain yourself. Now."

"Instead of going to school this morning, I got a ride to the bus station, bought a ticket to Durango and here I am."

Closing her eyes, Dana pressed a palm against her forehead. "Whoa, whoa. Let me guess. Your cousin Jessica drove you to the bus station and helped you buy a ticket, didn't she? Does Aunt Jennifer know about this little trip?"

"N-not yet. Jessica's going to tell her when I don't come

home from school, and I've been texting Jess on my cell phone all the way down here. But none of that's important, Mom."

"You're right." Dana blew out a breath. At least Kelsey had gotten here safely and as long as she stayed put at the bus depot until Dana picked her up, everything would be fine.

Except that Kelsey and her father would be in the same city at the same time.

"Don't be mad, Mom. I had to come. I—I sensed you were in danger. I had a dream."

Dana's heart resumed its thudding, the blood pounding in her ears. "What kind of dream?"

Kelsey sighed. "You know. The kind of dream I had when I was little. The kind of dream you told me to forget about. The kind of dream I still have…but never tell you about anymore."

Dana sagged against one of the stone posts in front of the cultural center as pinpricks of fear needled her back.

Her daughter was a Redbird.

That fact hadn't escaped Dana's notice when she gave birth to a baby girl. She'd watched her toddler for signs of the gift, just as surely as a mother would watch for signs of some horrible genetic disease in her child. When Kelsey had spoken of dreams during the day or intense feelings about a particular situation, Dana had coaxed, wheedled and trained those responses out of her daughter.

Or at least she thought she had.

The fear morphed into a crushing guilt. She'd only ended up teaching Kelsey to hide her feelings. Perhaps to fear them. Be ashamed of them. Like she had been ashamed. Now she had to reassure Kelsey…reassure her and send her home.

"Honey, don't worry. I'm not in any danger. I'm just doing my job." *Yeah, that and a little abracadabra on the side.*

"I had the feeling so strong yesterday afternoon. I couldn't think about anything else."

Yesterday afternoon Dana had been holding hands with a corpse, reliving her murder. She had to get Kelsey out of here. "Stay right where you are. I'm coming to pick you up."

Dana burst into the cultural center, begging a ride from Ben back to Auntie Mary's. As Ben ducked into his office to retrieve his keys, Lenny moseyed to the front door.

"I can give you a lift in my old blue Grand Prix. I'd like to pay my respects to Auntie Mary."

"She can live without that." She spun on her heel and threw open the door to wait for Ben.

Once Ben dropped her off, Dana poked her head inside the house to tell Auntie Mary about Kelsey and then retrieved her car.

On the drive to Durango, Dana called her cousin Jennifer to give her the news. After the conversation, she had a feeling Jessica would be losing driving privileges for a while.

Dana pulled up in front of the squat beige building with her mouth dry, even though she'd kept Kelsey on the phone almost the entire trip. She expelled a breath when her daughter tripped through the glass doors of the bus station, a hot pink backpack slung over one shoulder.

Dana popped the locks on the rental and Kelsey clambered into the car, suffocating her mother with a big hug. "I'm sorry, Mom. I promise I won't do this again, but I'm happy you're okay."

Inhaling Kelsey's peach-scented shampoo, Dana patted her on the back and kissed the side of her head. "I'm happy you're okay too. Why didn't you just call if you thought I was in danger? You didn't have to climb on a bus."

Kelsey hunched her shoulders and slanted a gaze in her direction. Guilt settled like a rock in Dana's stomach. She'd made it clear to Kelsey that she didn't want to hear about the gift, wanted to pretend it didn't exist. She knew better now, and her guilt encompassed more than just her behavior toward her daughter.

If Dana had developed her gift instead of fighting it, she might have more than just an image of a crown to help law enforcement nail the Headband Killer.

The Headband Killer. She had to get Kelsey out of Silverhill as quickly as possible.

"I had to see for myself that you were okay. Can you come home now?" Kelsey's hands formed small fists and Dana knew seeing wasn't necessarily believing for Kelsey.

Dana brushed Kelsey's arm with her fingertips before maneuvering onto the highway. "You know I can't do that, honey. Not until my job is done."

"What's the job this time?"

Dana had tried to keep Kelsey as far away from her investigations as possible. Gift or no gift, she wasn't about to start filling her in now.

"Just another bad guy to catch. And we're close."

"Do you think Auntie Mary will be mad?"

"I already told her and she'll be thrilled to see you. Tell you what. You can stay the weekend and go to the opening of the Southern Ute Cultural Center on Saturday night."

Dana gnawed on her lower lip. Her plans for telling Rafe about Kelsey after the investigation just blew up in her face. She'd have to come clean now. He'd be at the debut of the cultural center too and she couldn't lie to his face. Not after last night.

Her cell phone buzzed, and she grabbed it from the console and glanced at the display. Rafe's cell. She tossed the phone into the cup holder. She needed time. She needed a plan.

She had to break the news to Rafe in the best way possible.

RAFE PRINTED OUT HIS LETTER to the State Board of Medical Examiners regarding Dr. Simpson's omission, and then kicked his feet up on his desk and leaned back in his chair.

Having Dana in his arms again felt like coming home. Not just because she'd been his first lover, but because she'd been his best and he didn't mean in the technical sense.

He never had to prove anything to Dana. She'd shrugged at the McClintock name, money and influence. She'd yawned at Rafe's athletic prowess and rolled her eyes at his antics. None of that stuff had impressed her. He figured he didn't stand a chance with the brainy, pretty Ute girl…until they took the same American lit class and she discovered he liked the writers of the American West—James Fenimore Cooper, Stephen Crane and Zane Grey, among others—as much as she did.

And then just like that, without resorting to the famous Rafe McClintock charm, he had her hooked. It stayed that way between them. She liked him for what he had on the inside.

When Mom left the family, like all kids, Rafe took the blame onto his own shoulders. He figured his mom never would've left if he'd been good enough, smart enough… enough.

He grinned. He'd been enough for Dana last night.

The station phone rang, and since Shelly was still out to lunch, Rafe picked it up. "Silverhill Sheriff's Station."

"Hey there, Sheriff. This is Lenny Driscoll."

"Yeah?" Rafe swung his legs off the desk, the front legs of his chair banging on the floor. A call from Driscoll always meant bad news.

"It's Dana."

Rafe sat up straight while his heart thumped against his rib cage. "What's wrong? What happened?"

"Don't go all six-gun sheriff on me. Dana's all right, but she needs to see you at Auntie Mary's house."

"Why?" Rafe took a swig of warm bottled water. He didn't trust Driscoll one bit, especially when it concerned Dana.

"Something happened at the cultural center. I think it's about the murder investigation. You know how she gets those funny feelings? It's a Redbird thing. I always wondered if she used the gift to solve crimes."

Rafe choked on the water, spraying his keyboard. Damn it. Driscoll did know about the gift, and he obviously knew Dana was tapping into it. How many people had he told already?

"Why are you telling me this? How come Dana didn't call?"

"Like I told you, I saw her at the cultural center. And I don't think she wants you to know about this."

Rafe cut him off and ended the call. While fumbling for his cell phone, he swept his keys off the desk and tipped his hat from the hook. He speed-dialed Dana's number while his boots crunched across the gravel to his squad car. No answer.

He tried her phone twice more on his way to the reservation with no luck. He loosened his grip on the steering wheel and flexed his fingers. Maybe she'd just found out the FBI decided to take over the case and the task force. Not that the idea of the fibbies moving in on his territory thrilled him, but it beat the thought that Dana faced some danger she didn't want to share with him.

He careened around the corner of Auntie Mary's house just

as the door on Dana's rental swung open and Dana climbed out of the car. Rafe released a noisy breath. She looked fine. In fact, she was laughing. Had Driscoll tricked him for some reason?

The passenger door opened and a young girl with long, dark hair got out of the car. Rafe skidded to a stop in front of the house, and Dana's head jerked around. Her mouth formed an *O,* wiping the smile off her face, her eyes mimicking the shape of her lips.

Rafe scrambled out of the car, leaving the door open behind him. "You okay?"

Dana's gaze darted to the girl and then back to him before she dropped her keys. She bent over to pick them up and gave a short laugh as she straightened. "Everyone's worried about me today."

The girl smiled while drawing straight dark brows over her nose. She resembled Dana—must be her cousin's daughter.

Rafe sauntered toward the car, hands shoved in his pockets, feeling foolish for allowing Driscoll to get under his skin. Driscoll probably just wanted to let him know his suspicions about Dana using the gift on this case. Maybe even wanted to blackmail them.

"Hi, there." Rafe smiled at the girl.

"Kelsey, this is…uh…Sheriff McClintock. Sheriff, this is Kelsey." Dana waved her hand between the two of them, her face flushed.

Kelsey extended her small, slender hand and Rafe took it in his. "Nice to meet you, Sheriff McClintock."

Good to see kids with manners these days. "Nice to meet you too, Kelsey. Are you Jennifer's girl?"

Dana sucked in a sharp breath at the same time the screen door banged open. The girl dropped Rafe's hand and squealed, "Auntie Mary!"

Auntie Mary's weathered face broke into a broad smile.

"I'm glad you got here safely. You come inside while the grown-ups talk business." She enfolded Kelsey in a big hug and pinned Dana with a dark look over the girl's head.

When the door closed, Rafe turned to Dana. "Cute girl. She looks like you and Jennifer."

Dana jiggled the car keys in her hand. Her dark eyes took up half of her face as she sucked in her lower lip. Maybe Driscoll was telling the truth for once.

"What are you doing here?" Dana's voice cracked as if she hadn't used it for a long time.

"You are okay, aren't you? I got a call from your stepfather, who said you found something at the cultural center and were in some kind of trouble."

"Lenny?" She dropped the keys again but didn't bother to pick them up this time.

"I was beginning to think it was all a crock, that he just wanted to gloat over the fact that he knows you're using the gift."

"He does?" Dana slumped against the car. "I—I was afraid he might figure it out. Is that all he told you?"

"Is there more?" He grabbed her ice-cold hand and chafed it between his. She didn't seem as upset by the news as he expected. But if word leaked out that Dana had decided to use her powers to track this killer, Rafe wanted her the hell out of Silverhill.

"There is more, Rafe." A few strands of hair clung to Dana's eyelashes, and she brushed her hand across her eyes.

He clenched his gut as if waiting for a fist to make contact. Did she have another vision? Did the Headband Killer already make a move?

She tugged at his hand. "Let's sit on the porch."

On legs that felt like stilts, he followed her to Auntie Mary's porch and dropped down beside her. Hunching his shoulders, he braced his hands on his knees.

Dana took a deep breath and shuddered as she let it out. "I picked up the girl you just met, Kelsey, at the Durango bus station. I think Lenny must've followed me and called you to intercept us here."

Rafe twisted his head around and fell against the wooden railing bordering the porch steps. The girl? He blinked. Was Dana tense over a family issue?

"Did Jennifer's daughter run away from home or something? What's that got to do with Lenny?"

Dana pressed her knees against the folded hands between them, her knuckles as white as the painted trim on Auntie Mary's windows. "Kelsey isn't my cousin's daughter. Jennifer's daughter, Jessica, is sixteen."

Rafe ran a hand beneath the band of his hat as if to clear the fog clouding his brain. The girl. Not Jennifer's daughter. Not sixteen. Younger. Ten? Eleven?

He shot to his feet, his hand grasping the post. "How old is Kelsey?"

"Kelsey will be ten in December."

Bits of conversation, images and photos all clicked into place like pieces of a puzzle. A puzzle of deception.

Rafe stumbled off the step and strode to his squad car. He hurled himself into the car, slammed the door and cranked on the engine.

He had to get away. He had to get away from her. She didn't call out to him. She didn't try to stop him. What could she say?

She'd kept his daughter from him for almost ten years.

Chapter Twelve

Dana rested her elbows back on the top step and, through a haze of tears, watched Rafe's car speed away. From her. From their daughter.

What had she expected?

The screen door creaked open behind her. Her aunt touched the top of her head. "Give him time."

Dana closed her eyes and leaned her head against Auntie Mary's legs. "He'll never forgive me. The betrayal in his eyes shattered my heart."

"He may not forgive you, but Rafe McClintock's going to want to know his daughter. And you have to allow that, whether or not he wants anything more to do with you. That's the price you pay for deception."

Auntie Mary's straight talk plunged the knife deeper into Dana's heart, but she knew her wise aunt spoke the truth. She'd advised Dana at the time to tell Rafe. Why had she allowed Rafe's spiteful stepmother to influence her decision more than her trusted aunt? She'd convinced herself that she'd lied to protect Rafe, but maybe her own selfishness drove her more than she cared to admit.

"Now get in there and tell your daughter about her father." Auntie Mary tugged Dana's hair.

"D-do you think I should do that now?" Dana pushed up from the porch on shaky legs.

Auntie Mary put her arm around Dana's waist. "You've wasted enough time. You don't want her to stumble across the truth like Rafe did. Tell her now, and then you can introduce them properly."

"I don't want her here for long. I told her she could attend the opening of the cultural center and then I'm sending her home. If Steve can spare me, I might even fly up with her. It's not safe for her while I'm working this case."

Auntie Mary nodded. "I know. This case isn't safe for you either. Kelsey told me why she came. She felt danger all around you."

"She told you that?"

"I feel it, too. And our feelings are more than vague hunches." Auntie Mary gripped Dana's wrists, her gnarled fingers biting into her flesh. "We're Redbird women."

THREE HOURS LATER, after burying his rage in piles of paper-work, Rafe squatted on the flat rock that hung over the Twirling Ballerinas. The fantastic rock formations resembled six ballerinas on their toes. He chucked a pebble at one of the dancers and cursed.

He had a daughter. Kelsey.

Why'd she do it? Why had Dana kept the truth from him all these years?

He laughed, the bitter sound creating a faint echo in the canyon. *Why do you think she kept it from you?* Irrespon-sibility, immaturity and clowning weren't exactly the perfect qualities for fatherhood.

Through the years he hadn't proved himself any more capable of caring for a daughter than he would've been at eighteen. In L.A. he'd worked hard and partied hard, trying to prove…what? That he could get lots of people to love him even if his own mother didn't?

He clenched his teeth against that pathetic truth and tossed another rock at a ballerina.

"Is that dancer meant to be me?"

He shifted a quick glance at Dana, clambering up to his perch, and then looked away. His jaw hardened and he tipped his hat over his face, blocking the blazing sunset from his vision.

As Dana gripped the edge to hoist herself onto the flat rock, Rafe curled his fingers into his thighs to prevent himself from helping her.

The toes of her running shoes scrabbled for a foothold, but she slid down a few feet. Rafe blew out a breath, leaned over and grabbed her arms, pulling her onto his lookout.

He dropped her wrists as soon as she stood beside him, and she wiped her forehead with the back of her hand. "Whew. Thanks for the lift. I'd forgotten how tough this final part of the trail could be."

Dana's breath came out in short gasps and she'd worked up a sweat, which only intensified the smell of her musky floral perfume. His gaze focused on the bits of rock on her palm, along with a few bloody streaks.

He pulled a handkerchief from his back pocket and circled her wrist with his fingers. Silently, he brushed the debris from her palm and blotted her scratches.

"Thanks." She closed a fist around the handkerchief and dropped her lashes. "I'm sorry, Rafe."

He bit back his angry retort and returned to his spot on the rock, dangling his legs over the edge. "What's she like?"

Settling next to him, Dana folded her legs beneath her. "She's smart, but she doesn't much like school. She'd rather play soccer. She once answered a story problem about asparagus on a math test by stating that she wouldn't have any asparagus left because she hated asparagus and would give away her share."

Rafe snorted. He'd always believed story problems were irrelevant in the grand scheme of life.

Dana's shoulder pressed against his as she continued. "Her teachers tell me she's the class clown, and I know she's popular. Other girls flock to her. She loves pizza and Rocky Road ice cream."

As the sun dipped behind a ridge of mountains, Dana told him about Kelsey—her likes and dislikes, her personality and her strengths and challenges. His heart filled with pride and emotion choked him, not the anger and betrayal he'd nursed all afternoon but something else…wonder.

"She sounds…"

"Just like you." Dana smoothed her hand down his back. "God knows she's nothing like her type A, rigid mother. And right now she's crazy impatient to meet her father."

"She knows?"

Dana folded her hands in her lap. Rafe had been receptive to hearing about his daughter, but he'd reserved the warmth in his voice for Kelsey. The eyes that met hers briefly as they talked flashed a cold light, like hardened steel. He'd remained unresponsive to her light touches.

He'd want to be involved in Kelsey's life, but he'd never forgive her mother.

"I told her after you left Auntie Mary's house. Naturally she was upset because I'd led her to believe her dad left us. Now she's just excited to see you." Dragging in a ragged breath, Dana staggered to her feet and stretched her arms to the sky.

"So are you interested in meeting your daughter…again?"

She held out a hand to Rafe, but he ignored it and jumped to his feet, brushing the dirt from the seat of his jeans.

"Did you think I'd turn away from her? Is that why you didn't bother to tell me about your pregnancy and then kept quiet for ten years?"

Dana opened her mouth, years of explanations and excuses and insecurities tumbling to her lips, but Rafe held up his hand.

"Save it."

Dana gulped back a sob, her eyes stinging with tears. She deserved his scorn. She crept to the edge of the lookout in the darkness.

A beam of light danced in front of her and Rafe said, "Hold on. I brought a flashlight."

He deftly climbed down the rock face, as sure-footed as a mountain lion, and jumped to the trail below. With one hand, he aimed his flashlight at the first foothold and he used the other to grab her calf, guiding her foot to the small crevice.

When she reached the bottom, Rafe placed his hands around her waist and lifted her down. Once he placed her on solid ground, he dropped his hands as if burned.

She had burned him…badly.

He gestured with his flashlight down the path. "I'll lead. You follow. Just be careful where the path narrows up ahead."

Dana knew that stretch of the trail, which plunged off into nothingness after a few detours over craggy rocks. When the trail narrowed, she slipped her hand beneath Rafe's shirt and hooked her fingers in his waistband. The warm skin of his back scorched her hand as she remembered caressing him there.

Had that just been last night? It seemed as long ago as the first time they made love in one of the caves not far from the trail they now traipsed over silently like two strangers.

His back stiffened at her touch but he didn't shrug her off.

When the trail opened up and leveled off, Dana maintained her hold on Rafe. He knew the way a lot better than she did, and she had no intention of obliging his anger toward her by falling off a cliff. So she continued to stumble along behind him.

Kelsey had been mad when Dana told her the man she met outside was her father. She'd cried and lashed out, and just like with Rafe's wrath, Dana accepted it all.

Then she'd bounced back and asked a million questions. She claimed she'd sensed something special about Rafe the minute he took her hand. And Dana believed her…because she had, too.

Dana had taken advantage of the situation by trying to convince Kelsey the danger she felt surrounding her mother concerned Rafe. Kelsey acted like she bought it, but she didn't fool Dana. Her daughter had a lot of practice concealing her true feelings from her mother.

They neared the end of the trail and Dana released her hold on Rafe. He shot ahead of her, already digging his keys from his pocket.

She didn't want him rushing over to Auntie Mary's without her. She quickened her steps, slipped and tumbled against a boulder at the side of the trail. She threw out her hands and landed on top of the big rock, scraping her palms and bumping her knee.

"Damn. Would you wait up?"

All at once the darkness of the night grew blacker and engulfed her on all sides. An overpowering fear clutched her heart like a fist and she fell back against the boulder.

She couldn't breathe. A pair of strong hands had her by the throat. She clawed at the hands encased in latex gloves. Thin latex. Using her long fingernails, she scratched at the gloves, poking and gouging.

She wanted to scratch him. She wanted to hurt him, but her

fingernails couldn't rip through the gloves. His left glove stretched tightly across a ring on his finger. She dragged her nail across the flat part of the ring. A tiny hole opened and she tried to widen it, but she felt light-headed. The pad of her finger skimmed across the ring and she felt the outline of a crown.

Rafe cradled her in his lap, holding her tightly, rocking back and forth.

Dana sputtered and coughed and then buried her head against his shirt. He stroked her hair and murmured in her ear, "I'm sorry I left you behind. I'm here now."

Dana raised her head and leaned her chin on Rafe's shoulder, gulping in deep breaths of pine-scented air. "I—I had another vision, Rafe."

"Shh. I know. I could tell from the posture of your body and the way your eyes rolled back. It was just like the other two times, but scarier. What happened? Why did you go into a trance?"

Shaking her head, Dana bit her lip and clung to Rafe more tightly. "I don't know why it happened."

She did know letting down her guard and giving in to her emotions created more susceptibility to the gift. Those scenes with Kelsey and Rafe had shaken her to the core and further hacked away at her peace of mind.

"What were you doing? What were you thinking?" Rafe smoothed the hair back from her brow.

Dana pursed her lips. She'd been thinking she wanted to smack Rafe for rushing ahead of her. Then she tripped. She'd tripped and fallen across the boulder.

A tingle raced up her spine. Her previous visions had all come after coming into contact with the victims, either directly or indirectly.

The last thing she remembered before the vision took control of her mind was her palms smacking against the rock where Rafe now sat with her curled up in his lap. She slid from his thighs, her bottom hitting the hard surface of the boulder. She tracked the grooves and ridges of the rock with her fingertips, which now buzzed at the contact.

Rafe cocked his head, raising one brow. "What is it?"

"I got the vision because I landed on this rock."

"What?" Rafe jumped from the rock as if it were a hot seat.

Dana splayed her fingers on the boulder and leaned forward. The granite seemed to come alive beneath her touch. Images and thoughts swirled in her head.

The crown. The gold crown belonged on a ring, not in someone's mouth or on someone's head.

She dragged her hands away from the rock and clapped them together. "That crown I flashed on last time with Jacey? It's imprinted on a ring. The killer wears a gold ring engraved with a crown on his left hand."

Rafe's jaw dropped before he swept her into a hug. "That's huge. It's the best clue we've gotten yet for this investigation."

"There's something else, Rafe." She grabbed the flashlight dangling from his hand and swept its beam across the boulder. "Something happened in this spot. That's why the vision hit me."

He snapped his fingers. "Lindy Spode. She had some pine needles in her hair that weren't consistent with the location of her body."

The victim murdered here hadn't seen her attacker. His hands came at her from behind while she was sitting on the boulder. Dana skirted the rock and pointed Rafe's flashlight at the ground behind it.

Rafe crouched beside her and peered at the blanket of pine needles and pebbles in the dirt. He asked her to shine the light on the tree that hung over the beginning of the trail, and then studied the bark and the low-hanging branches.

"It's hard to see anything in this light. We'll have to send a forensics team out here to look for evidence."

"What excuse are we going to give them?"

Rafe dropped to his haunches and stirred the needles with a pen. "I'll say I got an anonymous tip. That's not too far from the truth."

Drawing in a quick breath, Rafe pinched a white object between his fingers and held it up to the light. "A cigarette butt."

"Who'd be crazy enough to smoke out here?"

"A nervous killer?" Rafe wrapped the butt in his handkerchief and stuck it in the pocket of his jacket.

"Lenny smokes."

"Yeah, but does he also have a gold ring with a crown on it?" Rafe gestured her back onto the trail and out to the road where they'd parked their cars.

"He must've parked his car right here to load the body in his trunk and take it to that construction site." He surveyed the gravel road that sat at the head of the Twirling Ballerinas Trail. "You know, this is where Zack Ballard was murdered by that maniac who was after my sister-in-law, Julia. We found his body sprawled across the trail."

Dana shivered and clutched her upper arms. "This trail is going to get a spooky reputation. There's something creepy about the legend of the frozen ballerinas anyway."

"I wonder why he doesn't just leave the bodies where he murders them. Why risk additional evidence by loading them in his trunk and dumping them in another location?"

"He wants us to discover them."

"Someone would've found Lindy here, and someone sure as hell would've seen Jacey's body in the Shopco parking lot. There's some significance about the construction sites."

"Maybe he's familiar with them." Dana hesitated before

climbing into her rental. "Are you going to follow me to Auntie Mary's? It's not too late."

"She…Kelsey won't be asleep?"

"It's only seven-thirty, and even if it were two o'clock in the morning I think she'd be waiting for you."

"How would I know about her bedtime?" He shrugged, a careless gesture that couldn't mask the pain in his eyes.

Pain she'd put there.

"I'm sure she's anxious to tell you about her bedtime and everything else, Rafe. She needs her father."

He blew out a breath and opened his car door. "Are you okay to drive?"

She assured him she was, and he followed her to Auntie Mary's house, the glow of his headlights soothing to her frazzled nerves.

When Dana pulled into her aunt's driveway, the front door flew open and Kelsey dashed outside. Before Dana even cut the engine, Kelsey was next to the car pulling at the door handle.

Fear pulsed through Dana's veins. Was Auntie Mary hurt?

She pushed open the car door and stood up, staggering back as Kelsey threw her arms around her waist, sobbing. With trembling fingers, Dana stroked her daughter's hair. "What is it? What happened?"

Rafe blew past them, shooting her a worried look over Kelsey's head. As he reached the porch, Auntie Mary stepped outside and waved her hands at him. "I'm fine. It's not me."

Dana cupped Kelsey's face in her hands. "What's wrong, honey?"

"Where were you, Mom? I was so scared."

Rafe had tripped back down the steps and stood by the car, his hands fisted at his sides.

Dana recognized that look on his face. He wanted to swoop

in and rescue them both, but he didn't want to move too quickly around Kelsey until he got to know her better. God, what a mess she'd made of it all.

Clicking her tongue, Dana swept a tear from Kelsey's cheek. "I'm okay. I went to find Sheriff McClintock…your father…to tell him all about you. He's as anxious to get to know you as you are to get to know him."

Kelsey stepped back into the curve of Dana's arm and her gaze narrowed as she focused on Rafe. "You were with *him?*"

The lines on Rafe's face deepened at Kelsey's cold tone, and Dana shook her daughter. "I told you, Kelsey. I said I was going to find your father and bring him back here to introduce the two of you properly. What's wrong with you?"

Kelsey wiped the back of her hand across her eyes and gripped Dana's hand. "You were with the bad man. The man who hurts girls."

Chapter Thirteen

His daughter's words punched him in the gut. She knew about the Headband Killer? And she'd already fingered him as the culprit? Not a great start to a father-daughter relationship.

"Dana, what is she talking about?"

Dana had stumbled back against the car door, still clutching Kelsey's hand. "You felt that? You knew I'd had contact with...with that man?"

"She started feeling agitated about an hour ago." Auntie Mary stepped off the porch. "I tried to calm her down, but she insisted you were in danger."

Rafe's throat tightened as the truth sucked the air out of his lungs. His daughter was a Redbird. She had the gift too.

Dana smoothed a thumb across Kelsey's cheek. "I wasn't in danger. I had a vision. You know how that works."

Kelsey sagged against her chest. "Yeah, I know how it works, but I have such strong feelings that you're in trouble, Mom. They won't go away."

"The vision scared me. I'm not accustomed to them, but Sheriff McClintock, your father, he helped me."

Kelsey turned her head and peered at Rafe through the long hair that hung over her face. "I didn't really think...I know you're not the bad man."

His lips quirked into a smile even though worry still gnawed at his gut. "That's okay. I'm protective of your mom too."

Auntie Mary clucked her tongue and herded everyone inside the house. "Now that we know you two have that in common, let's find out what else you share."

RAFE THREW HIS FILES in his desk drawer and locked it. He grabbed his hat from the hook on the wall, hesitating as the phone rang. He called back to Brice, "You got that?"

"I'm on it." Brice waved at Rafe to leave, but Rafe stopped with his hand on the doorknob.

"Silverhill Sheriff's Department." Brice paused. "The fight's still going on?"

Rafe crossed his arms over his chest, leaning against the door. Sounded like they might have to lock someone up in the tank.

Rolling his eyes, Brice covered the mouthpiece of the phone with his hand. "Fight at the Elk between Lenny Driscoll and Joshua Trujillo."

Rafe raised his brows. Driscoll was getting a little old for bar fights, and Trujillo always struck him as a lover not a fighter. Must be booze, gambling or both.

"We'll be right over, Chuck." Brice shoved back from his desk and grabbed his keys. "You can take off, Sheriff. I know you have…things to do."

Did everyone in town know he and Dana had a daughter? He opened the door and gestured Brice through. "If this involves Driscoll and alcohol, you're going to need backup."

By the time Rafe and Brice raced the few blocks to the Elk, other customers had broken up the fight and were restraining the two men, who glared and cursed at each other.

During the fight, the men had managed to knock over a

couple of chairs and a potted plant. A few broken glasses littered the floor along with some playing cards.

Rafe settled between the two combatants with a wide stance, and their captors released them. "What's the problem? I sure hope there wasn't any gambling going on here. That's illegal activity, even on the reservation."

Lenny wiped his bloody mouth with his sleeve and grinned. "Just a friendly game, Sheriff. A friendly game I won fair and square."

"You're a cheater." Joshua lunged at Lenny and Rafe stopped him with a hand to the chest. "Hold it. Someone tell me what happened, or I'm hauling both of you into the station."

"I was playing some cards with some buddies." Lenny jerked his thumb over his shoulder at the upended table. "Just a few small wagers, Sheriff, no big deal. This boy here wanted in on the game and started losing pretty big."

"It was a setup. You were cheating from the start."

Rafe held up his hands. "Does Joshua owe you money, Lenny? Because if that's the case, you'd better walk away now while you're ahead."

"Oh, I got paid, Sheriff." Lenny winked. "I don't deal a card until I see the cold, hard cash…or something else…on the table."

"C'mon Joshua." Rafe took the other man by the arm. "Let it go now."

Joshua shrugged him off. "You don't get it, Rafe. How could you? You're not Ute and neither is Driscoll, even though you both like to steal our women."

Lenny laughed, which heightened Joshua's color even more until he looked ready to go after Lenny…or him.

"That's enough." Gritting his teeth, Rafe put a hand on Joshua's back and steered him toward the door. "Why are you worried about the stench of gambling now when you wanted to put a casino on the reservation?"

Joshua grabbed onto the doorjamb. "It's not the gambling, it's what I lost. I didn't lose money to Lenny. I lost one of the seven sacred rings."

Rafe dropped his hand from Joshua's back. "A ring?"

He glanced at Lenny, now tossing a bright gold object in the air.

"It's mine now, baby." Lenny smirked. "And don't start spouting that crap about your sacred Ute traditions. Ben tried to get you to donate the ring to his cultural center and you were holding out for the highest bidder."

Joshua clenched his fists. "Is that why you tricked me out of the ring? You're going to sell it to Ben?"

Rafe's gaze tracked the ring as Lenny flicked it up and then snatched it in his hand over and over. He thrust out his own hand. "Let me see that ring."

The tone of Rafe's voice wiped the smile off Lenny's face. "I won this ring, Sheriff. I have witnesses."

"Give it over." Rafe cupped his hand and crooked his finger.

Lenny dropped the heavy ring in Rafe's palm. Pinching it between his fingers, Rafe turned the ring over and a fast pulse beat in his throat. The ring had a gold crown imprinted on its face.

The ring of a killer.

Running the pad of his thumb across the crown, his gaze shifted between Joshua's tight-jawed face and Lenny's scowling one. Unknown to both of them, they'd just become suspects in the Headband Killer case. He had to show this ring to Dana.

He closed his fist around the ring. "I'm holding on to this for now."

Both men's voices erupted in protest.

Rafe tilted his chin toward the bar. "Drunk in public, public nuisance, assault, destruction of property. I'm taking this ring as evidence, and you'd both better hope I don't decide to haul you in and charge you."

Joshua stormed out of the bar and Lenny sauntered after him.

Chuck thanked Rafe, and he and a couple of his customers began picking up the chairs and sweeping the glass.

Brice asked, "What are you going to do with the ring? Driscoll may have won the ring at cards, but I'm sure he cheated if Joshua said so."

Rafe dropped the ring in the pocket of his jacket. "I'm going to keep it until those two hotheads cool off. Then we'll figure it out."

He and Dana hadn't told anyone in their respective departments about the ring, not even Emmett. How could they explain that the mark on the victims' necks had come from a gold ring with a crown on it? Even after giving that hint to Dr. Simpson, he hadn't come to any conclusions about it.

As Rafe dropped off Brice at the station, his cell phone buzzed.

Dana's guarded voice came over the line, "Are you still coming over for dinner?"

Guess she still couldn't quite believe he had an interest in getting to know his daughter. He must've put on one convincing act that he didn't want anything to do with family or kids way back when. Had Dana really taken an eighteen-year-old kid that seriously?

"I'm on my way, but I need to see you before we go into the house. Business. Watch for my squad car and meet me out front."

Twenty minutes later, Rafe pulled in front of Auntie Mary's

house, the ring burning a hole in his pocket. As soon as he stopped the car, Dana rushed down the front steps, casual in jeans and a sweater.

He powered down the window. "Hop inside."

She drew her dark brows together, but walked around to the passenger side and slid into the car. "This must be important."

Rafe scooped the ring from his pocket, opening his hand as he extended it to her.

Dana gasped, "That's the ring. Where'd you get it?"

"I don't want to tell you yet."

She reached for the ring, but he snatched back his hand. "No."

"Are you crazy?"

He'd seen this one coming and while he knew she'd win, he wanted to delay the inevitable. "Not now."

Taking a deep breath, she gripped his arm. "You know as well as I do, we can't waste time. What if he strikes tonight? What if he's stalking somebody right now?"

Not likely, since he had his guy on patrol watching Lenny and Joshua was on his way to one of his clubs in Durango. But Dana didn't have to know any of that yet. He didn't want her vision tainted with prior knowledge.

Rafe uncurled his fingers and the ring picked up the light from Auntie Mary's porch and glinted in his palm.

"That's better." Dana plucked the ring from his hand, traced the crown with her fingertip and then squeezed the ring in her fist. Leaning her head back, she closed her eyes.

Rafe held his breath. He studied her face while he clutched the steering wheel as if ready for takeoff. Only she'd be the one to take off, not him.

Her steady breathing filled the car. Her lashes fluttered, and Rafe ground his teeth together. Maybe this would be the last time she'd have to go through this.

"Damn." Her eyelids flew open, and she shook the ring in her hand. "Nothing."

"What do you mean, nothing?" He swallowed around the lump in his throat.

"I'm not getting anything from this ring—no feelings at all. Nothing."

"Could it be because it changed hands?"

"I don't know." She sighed. "I don't know the rules of this game or if there even are any rules."

"Don't you think it's about time we told your aunt what's going on with you? Now that Kelsey's here, it's not just about you anymore."

"Maybe you're right." She handed the ring back to him. "Do you want to tell me where you got it now?"

"It belonged to Joshua Trujillo. He lost it playing cards with Lenny."

"Oh, my God. Joshua?" She covered her mouth, her eyes wide above her hand. "Did you check out his alibi after you questioned him about interviewing Lindy for a job at his club?"

"Believe me, I'm going to go through his file with a magnifying glass tomorrow. But tonight I'm going to spend some time with my daughter before she has to go back to Denver."

They reached Auntie Mary's front door and Dana pushed it open, poking her head inside. "I hope you didn't start dinner without us."

Auntie Mary came out of the small kitchen, wiping her hands on a dish towel, with Kelsey close on her heels. "We waited. Kelsey helped me set the table."

Kelsey directed them to their places, putting herself opposite Rafe. The discovery of the ring had temporarily reduced Rafe's anxiety over this meeting with his daughter. Now the lump returned to his throat and even the mouthwatering smell of the beef stew couldn't jump-start his appetite. Even worse, Kelsey's steady gaze had him picking at the meat and shoving the vegetables around his plate as if he was a five-year-old.

Kelsey obviously suffered no such anxiety. She chewed vigorously as she sized him up. Suddenly, she dropped her fork and Rafe jumped. "We don't look much alike, do we?"

"Well—" Rafe wiped his napkin across his mouth "—you look very much like your mom."

Kelsey sighed. "I know. People tell me that all the time."

"You and your dad have the same mouth, the same smile." Dana rubbed Kelsey's arm. "I know that because you both smile a lot."

Kelsey flashed her white teeth in a big grin, and Rafe responded with the identical grin. They both laughed, a similar sound of unbridled joy. The knot in Rafe's chest vanished and his appetite returned.

He and his daughter spent the rest of the meal chatting and getting to know each other. They had a similar outlook on life, which both pleased and alarmed Rafe. Kelsey definitely didn't possess her mother's serious, studious nature. Kelsey had a carefree attitude, which probably allowed her, at the tender age of nine, to jump on a bus for a seven-hour journey to Durango.

Scary stuff, this parenting business.

The meal ended and Kelsey's bedtime rolled around sooner than Rafe expected or wanted.

Kelsey got ready for bed and Dana came out of the bedroom with a smile from ear to ear. "Kelsey wants you to tuck her in."

Rafe swallowed. Nine-year olds got tucked in? And what exactly did tucking in entail? "Sure."

He crept into the darkened room, a bedside lamp throwing a small pool of light on Kelsey's face. "I suppose you're too old for a bedtime story?"

"Yeah, I can read myself." She wrinkled her nose. "But I don't like to read."

"I gathered that from our conversation." He sat on the edge of her bed. "Maybe when you get a little older, I'll loan you a couple of Mark Twain books. His stories are funny and full of adventure. You might like him."

Kelsey surveyed him through narrowed eyes. "Maybe. You're mad at Mom, aren't you?"

"Not mad exactly, maybe a little upset." Rafe rubbed his palms on his jeans. So much for having a shy, sweet little girl.

"Does that mean you're going to go away?" She plucked at the bedcovers. "Does that mean you don't want to see us anymore?"

Rafe grabbed her small hands and chafed them between his. "No. However I feel about your mom, you're my daughter. I still have a lot to learn about you. I like you."

He bit his tongue. Should he have said love? He loved her already. How could he not?

Kelsey's wide grin split her face. "I like you too…Sheriff."

Rafe exhaled. He'd made the right move. He didn't want to rush her. He made a big deal out of tucking the covers around Kelsey and turning off the lamp. Then he kissed the top of her head and tiptoed out of the room.

When he walked into the living room, Dana met his gaze with a crease between her brows. "How'd it go?"

Guess his ability to be a father still concerned her. "I don't think my visit is going to give her nightmares, if that's what you mean."

"That's not what I mean. It's clear you two are like peas in a pod." She laced her fingers together and clenched her hands. "I told Auntie Mary about my visions."

His gaze darted to Auntie Mary's face, creased with worry. "And?"

Auntie Mary took a sip of hot tea before she answered. "And I think you two should've come to me sooner. Dana is inexperienced in the use of the gift, which could lead to real trouble."

"Did you tell Auntie Mary about the ring?"

Dana shook her head. "I didn't get to that part yet."

Dana explained how she felt the ring on the killer's finger, and that Rafe had just confiscated a ring that had been the subject of a bet between Lenny and Joshua Trujillo and that Dana had identified it as the same ring the killer wore when he had strangled his victims.

Auntie Mary had gone very still and clutched her cane in front of her. "What kind of ring is this? Can you describe it to me?"

"We can do better than that." He pulled the ring from his pocket, leaned forward and handed it to Auntie Mary.

She slipped it over the first knuckle of her gnarled index finger and held it in front of her. "I know all about this ring. It's one of the seven sacred rings."

Seven sacred rings. Dana squeezed her eyes shut, biting her lower lip. "Why does that sound familiar to me?"

"There was a time when you actually listened to the old stories." Auntie Mary shook her finger at Dana, and the ring glinted in the firelight. "When the Spanish began to come into Ute land, they were eager to make peace with the Ute. One of the Spanish conquistadors brought seven rings with him from King Philip, and the Spanish leader gave a ring to the head of each of the seven Ute groups that existed at the time."

Dana chastised herself once again for trying to shut out the mysticism of her culture. Instead of running from it, she should have been handing it down to Kelsey. Maybe Kelsey would be safe at home now if Dana hadn't tried so hard to squelch her daughter's natural gift.

"I remember." Dana shifted on the sofa to face Rafe. "Before each of the chiefs accepted the ring from the Spaniards, the group's shaman endowed the ring with special powers through charms and incantations. Do I have that right, Auntie Mary?"

"You do."

Rafe scratched his chin. "Seven rings? Where are the rest of them now?"

Auntie Mary ran her thumb across the face of the ring in a caress. "Ben Whitecotton has most of them."

Dana's heart skipped a beat. "Ben? Why does he have them?"

"Various people have donated them to the cultural center."

That argument she'd interrupted between Ben and Joshua made sense now. Ben probably wanted the ring from Joshua for the cultural center and Joshua had refused. Why? Did he have other uses for it?

Rafe asked, "How many of the remaining six rings does Ben have for the cultural center?"

"I'm not sure." Auntie Mary slipped the ring off her finger and held it out to Rafe. "I know he has more than one because we discussed placement of the rings in the display area of the center. Ask him."

"No." Rafe dropped the ring back in his pocket. "I don't want it to get out that we have a sudden interest in these rings."

Dana jumped from the sofa and stood with her back to the fireplace to get rid of the sudden chill in her bones. "I'll ask him tomorrow night at the opening celebration, where it will seem like a natural question."

"That's an excellent idea, Agent Croft."

"W-will you be there?"

"Of course. I helped Ben plan security. Rod and I are going over together. By the way, if this ring belongs to the killer, how come Dana isn't getting any vibes from it?"

Auntie Mary struggled to her feet and collected the cups on the table. "Either that's not the ring the killer was wearing or she's too tuned in to the victims to identify with the killer. That would explain why she's not getting any vibes, as you call it, from the killer himself."

Dana had sidled closer to him so that her shoulder brushed his. So close Rafe felt a ripple run through her body.

With eyes wide, she asked, "What do you mean by that?"

Auntie Mary spread her arms. "Let's face it. Silverhill is a small town and the reservation is even smaller. The killer is someone we know."

Chapter Fourteen

On his way to pick up Rod for the cultural center opening, Rafe stomped up the kitchen steps of the big house. A chorus of angry voices greeted him. Guess the honeymoon period had ended. He'd already told his family about Kelsey, but warned they wouldn't have a chance to meet her on this visit. Now he was glad.

He eased open the door and stuck his head inside. "Is it safe?"

They all snapped their mouths shut. Pam buried her tear-stained face in her hands as Dad's arm curled around her shoulder.

Scowling, Rod tossed a packet of papers on the kitchen table. "You'd better tell Rafe…everything."

Rafe quirked his eyebrow. "If this has anything to do with the ranch or money or Dad's retirement, I'll take a pass."

"It does have to do with all that." Rod crossed his arms over his chest and leaned one hip against the kitchen counter. "But it also involves you, Dana and that little girl of yours."

A muscle twitched in Rafe's jaw as he glanced at Pam, still huddled in her husband's embrace. "Okay, maybe I won't take a pass. Spill."

"We have a half brother."

Rafe's heart hammered in his chest. Had Rod found Mom? Would they finally see her again? "Mom?"

Rod snorted. "Are you kidding? The illegitimate brother is a McClintock, and Dad plans to ease his conscience by handing over the south property to him."

Rafe should've figured the bastard son belonged to Dad. He ran a hand across his mouth. "How old is he?"

"A year older than you, and a year younger than Ryder. Who cares? How am I supposed to carry through with the plans for the ranch without that property?"

Ralph sighed. "I have to do right by the boy. He's a McClintock."

"Yeah, like Pam tried to do right by Dana and that little girl?"

Rod's words cause another wave of sniffles from Pam, and Rafe clenched his stomach. "What are you talking about?"

"After Dad broke the news to me about our half brother, I stormed out of here but I came back. That's when I overheard Pam talking about Dana and Kelsey. I guess discussing one surprise baby brought up fond memories of another surprise baby."

"What the hell do you mean?" Rafe didn't give a damn about some half brother or the ranch, but Pam just might hold the key to why Dana kept her pregnancy a secret from him.

Rod leveled a finger at Pam. "I think she needs to explain what happened ten years ago when she discovered Dana's pregnancy."

"You knew Dana was pregnant?" A flash of heat seized his body and Rafe jerked his head toward Pam.

Dad patted her shoulder as she continued to sob. "Now, now. Pam did what she thought was best for the family—for you, Rafe and maybe even Dana."

Rafe gritted his teeth. He knew Pam would do what was

best for Pam. "What happened? How did you find out about Dana's pregnancy and what did you say to her?"

Pam waved her hands. "How I found out isn't important. But the advice I gave her saved you heartache, Rafe. That girl had big plans and dreams. Do you think she would've stuck around here to raise a baby with you? Do you think she would've followed you to L.A. and given up her scholarship?"

"None of that matters." Rafe smacked the kitchen table. "Those were our decisions to make, not yours. What did you tell her to make her agree to keep the baby a secret?"

"I didn't have to do much convincing. In her mind, she was halfway to Georgetown anyway…without you."

"Tell him, Pam." Rod hunched over the table, a dark, menacing look twisting his features.

Pam clutched her husband's hand. "I told her everyone would think she was just like her mother, Ronnie, trying to sleep her way into one of Silverhill's wealthy families."

Rafe clenched his fists. Pam had played on one of Dana's greatest fears. She'd used and manipulated a frightened eighteen-year-old girl.

Rod spit out, "Go on."

"I also told her that once Ralph found out about the baby, he'd disinherit you, cut you out of the family."

Rafe's gaze darted to his father's tired face. The man didn't look capable of such a Machiavellian scheme, but Rafe knew better.

"Hold on." Rod gripped Rafe's shoulder. "Dad didn't know anything about Dana's pregnancy. Pam didn't need to tell him because her ploy worked. Dana left town without a backward glance. The ironic thing is how this all came to light. Apparently, Dad threatened to take his bastard son away from his mother, so she took off. I overheard Pam and Dad reminiscing about their various plots concerning McClintock babies. Kind of gives you a warm and fuzzy, doesn't it?"

Kind of made Rafe want to punch a hole in the wall.

Why didn't Dana tell him about his stepmother's threats? Dana had shouldered the guilt on her own. Even if Pam's warning was an empty one, Dana couldn't have known that. She knew enough about how Ralph McClintock wielded power over his family to take Pam's promise seriously.

"Why'd you do it? Why'd you conspire to keep Dana and my child away from me?"

Pam held out her hand. "I did it for you, Rafe. You didn't need to be saddled with a wife and a baby at your age, especially a wife with a family like hers—Ronnie Croft was trash and her husband no better. Lenny Driscoll is still trash. I didn't want one little mistake to ruin your life."

"Because my life was so damn perfect?"

Rafe slammed out of the kitchen, heated blood thrumming through his veins. Dana had left out of some misplaced fear for him. Instead of blaming her, he should be apologizing for his screwed-up family. No wonder this mysterious half brother and his mother had disappeared.

Rod caught up with him and yanked open the passenger door of his truck. "Are you still giving me a ride to the cultural center?"

Rafe gunned the engine. "Didn't think you wanted to go after the bombshell. When did you find out about all this anyway?"

"About a half an hour before you stumbled into the kitchen."

Shaking his head, Rafe maneuvered out the front gates of the McClintock ranch. "Dad's a piece of work. Where is this half brother?"

"His wife's a piece of work too, and that's the million-dollar question. Where's the missing McClintock?"

Rafe slanted a glance toward his stoic older brother and a

shaft of sympathy passed through him. Rod deserved the ranch, the whole ranch. He'd worked hard for it and had put up with a lot more crap from Dad than he and Ryder could ever bear. "Look, I'm sorry about the south property."

"Forget it."

Case closed. Other than that flare-up of anger in the kitchen, Rod would never again reveal what he felt about this interloping McClintock brother...half brother.

"So I guess Dana never told you the real reason why she left town without a word about her pregnancy."

"She gave me the line that she did it for my own good, but she never told me about Pam's scare tactics. She never mentioned Pam. Dana took all the blame."

"Are you going to give Dana a chance? Looks like she took off to save you from family ostracism."

Rafe turned up the radio. Two could play that game. He didn't want to admit to Rod that he didn't know if Dana wanted a chance with him. She wanted a father for Kelsey, but did she want a husband for her bed?

He was the man for both jobs.

Rafe didn't bother Rod with any more questions about their half brother or the ranch and Rod mimicked his silence. By the time Rafe pulled into the parking lot of the new Southern Ute Cultural Center, the brothers had both had plenty of time to mull over their difficulties.

He didn't know about Rod, but Rafe planned to take action tonight. He hated the idea of Pam's lies snatching away decisions that rightfully belonged to him.

He controlled his destiny.

DANA LOOKED UP and spotted two tall men, one with a white cowboy hat and one with a black one, enter the room. As always, Rafe's appearance took her breath away, just like the first time she saw him in a crowded hallway at Silverhill High. Rod split off from Rafe and grabbed a beer from a roving waiter on his way to a group of his friends.

Rafe scanned the crowd until his gaze locked onto hers. They maintained eye contact as Rafe cut a path through the guests. His blue eyes still burned with intensity, but something else had replaced the anger of the past few days. Determination? Resolve?

A slow, sinuous flame curled through Dana's body, and she grasped her aunt's arm for support.

"Don't you think so, Dana?"

Dana jerked her head toward Ben Whitecotton, his brows raised in question. "I'm sorry. I didn't hear you."

Ben pursed his lips. "I asked if you thought it was a good idea to have Mary Redbird seated in the front of the room while I gave my presentation. Then she can be available to answer questions."

"Certainly, if she feels up to it."

"Daddy!" Kelsey wrapped her arms around Rafe's waist as he joined their circle.

Watching Rafe's face break into a smile as he ruffled Kelsey's hair, Dana's nose tingled and tears stung her eyes. Kelsey knew she had a gem of a father. Would Rafe ever forgive her and want to be more than Kelsey's father?

Rafe shook hands with Ben and kissed Auntie Mary's cheek. "Sorry to interrupt. Congratulations on the opening, Ben. Everything looks great. I trust security is in place?"

"Thanks to you, Rafe, security is running smoothly. And I believe congratulations are in order for you on the discovery of your daughter."

"Thanks. We have a lot of catching up to do." Rafe

pinched the end of Kelsey's nose. "Rod and I got a late start. Did I miss anything?"

Although he directed his question to Ben, Dana knew Rafe meant it for her. She hadn't had a chance to ask Ben about the rings yet. In fact, she hadn't even gotten close to the display case, even though every one of her nerve endings had been buzzing ever since she stepped through the doors to the cultural center. And Kelsey had been jumpier than a frog on a trampoline.

"No, you haven't missed a thing except this crushing crowd. We haven't even had an opportunity to look around at the displays yet."

Ben rubbed his hands together. "I'm going to give my talk in a few minutes. I'll direct everyone's attention to the different displays and give a short overview of the artifacts we have. Then we'll adjourn to the patio out back where we'll watch a performance of the Bear Dance."

"What's the Bear Dance, Mom?"

"You've been remiss in your daughter's education." Ben wagged his finger at Dana.

"If that means she doesn't teach me stuff, you're wrong." Kelsey planted her fists on her hips.

"Kelsey!" Dana cheeks burned at Kelsey's rudeness.

Rafe laid his hand on Kelsey's shoulder. "Young lady, you owe Mr. Whitecotton an apology right now."

Kelsey apologized to Ben, who waved it off. Then he and Rafe pulled a chair to the right of the podium and Ben tested his microphone.

Dana settled Auntie Mary in the chair. "I don't know what's gotten into Kelsey. She's usually not rude to adults like that."

"She's skittish tonight, isn't she? And I don't think it's just excitement over having a new father."

"I feel it too, don't you?" Dana laid her aunt's cane across her lap.

Auntie Mary closed her eyes. "I've been feeling it ever since the first murder. Maybe even before."

"May I have your attention please?" Ben tapped the side of the podium and gradually the chatter and laughter settled into a low murmur. "I'd like to welcome you all to the Southern Ute Cultural Center, made possible by the grant from Colrad Oil and your generous donations."

When the applause died down, Ben launched into the history of the cultural center, and then moved clockwise around the glass cases in the room to discuss each grouping of items on display.

As he approached one case he gestured to Auntie Mary, still seated near the podium. "We have Mary Redbird to thank for many of the items in this display of our mystical heritage. As many of you know, shamans in our particular grouping of the Ute tribe are women. Mary Redbird's mother was a powerful shaman in her day, and passed the gift along to Auntie Mary and her sister, Fanny. And then Fanny passed the gift to her daughter, Ronnie. And Ronnie…?"

Ben smiled at Dana, tilting his chin toward her.

Rafe cursed under his breath, and Dana rolled her bottom lip forward in a pout and shook her head. "I'm afraid the gift skipped me or petered out."

One of Auntie Mary's cronies coughed and cleared her throat. "You have to embrace the gift, my child. You're a Redbird woman. You have the gift within you."

The crowd shuffled and Dana felt everyone's gaze burning into her. Did one of those pairs of eyes belong to a killer?

Rafe stepped in front of Dana as if to shield her from the

inquiring and speculative stares. "What's that hanging on the wall behind the case, Ben?"

Ben moved on with his overview, and Dana expelled a long breath. Rafe reached back and squeezed her hand. He might still be angry with her over her deception, but his protective instincts always kicked in at the right moment.

Just as Dana's muscles began to relax, Ben reached the display case containing the sacred rings. Dana held her breath.

Rafe whispered in her ear, "This is it."

"Most of you know the story of the sacred rings of the Ute tribe. By the time the conquistadores charged onto our land, we had divided into seven groups, occupying seven different areas. Eager to trade with the Ute and make peace with us, the Spaniards offered a gold ring from their king to each of the chiefs of the seven tribes."

Rafe murmured, "Is he being particularly long-winded or is it just me?"

"I think it's just us."

Kelsey had taken a step back, crowding closely against Dana's and Rafe's legs. She reached up and grabbed Dana's hand with cold fingers.

Ben tapped the top of the display case. "We've been very lucky. We currently have five of the sacred rings."

Five rings and Rafe had one more in his possession from the bar fight between Lenny and Joshua. Dana glanced down as Kelsey's grip tightened. With her other hand Kelsey had slid her fingers into Rafe's pocket.

Ben unlocked the case and reached inside to slide one of the rings from its stand. "I'm in negotiations to get one more ring on loan, which will give us six of the original rings."

A soft whine escaped Kelsey's lips, and Rafe patted the top

of her head. Puzzled, Dana looked down, but Kelsey had dropped her head forward, her long hair hiding her face.

Someone from the audience called out, "Where's the seventh ring, Ben?"

Ben lifted his hands, balancing the ring on one palm. "Unfortunately, we simply do not know the location of the seventh ring."

Kelsey's body jerked and began trembling. Dana gasped and Rafe fell to his knees in front of Kelsey and gripped her shoulders.

Moaning, Kelsey closed her eyes and tilted back her head as she hugged herself. Her eyelids began fluttering, and Dana knelt beside Rafe and clutched Kelsey's stiff hand.

As her fingers closed around Kelsey's, an electric current coursed through Dana's body and violent images flashed through her brain. Kelsey's vision became hers. Dana blocked it with every technique she'd perfected over the years— blocked it for herself and for her daughter.

Rafe whispered, "Let's keep this quiet and get her out of here."

Dana's heart galloped with fear. This had to stop…now. She couldn't allow this vision to take control of Kelsey's mind. She pushed Rafe aside and shook Kelsey by the shoulders. "Kelsey!"

The crowd murmured and parted around them.

Dana plucked some ice out of her drink and ran it over Kelsey's cheeks. Kelsey bucked against her, and then her body went limp and she choked out a sob.

"Is everything okay?" Ben took a step forward, closing his hand around the ring.

Rafe scooped up Kelsey in his arms, clutching her to his chest. "Kelsey's not feeling well. I'll take her outside."

While she followed Rafe's solid form outside, Dana shot a worried glance at Auntie Mary, who held a finger to her lips.

Rafe settled Kelsey on a bench bordering the dance circle and held her hand as he smoothed her hair back from her forehead. "It's okay. You're safe now."

Kelsey whimpered as she clung to her newfound father. No doubt finding the same strength and reassurance in his low voice that Dana discovered years ago.

After several minutes, Kelsey sniffled and wiped her eyes. "I felt weird, Mom. I saw scary pictures in my head."

"Try to forget about it, honey. It's not important."

"I'll take her to get a fruit punch, and then you need to take her home." Auntie Mary had joined them on the patio, leaning heavily on her cane.

"I'm not a baby." She tilted her chin. "I—I want to stay and watch the Bear Dance."

Rafe pinched her earlobe. "You can see the Bear Dance another time. You know, I'm not a baby either, but I'm really tired and I'd like to leave. Will you let me take you back to Auntie Mary's? I think your mom should stay here with Auntie Mary, since she's the guest of honor."

Kelsey's eyes brightened and a little color crept back into her cheeks. "Okay. Can I have a fruit punch first and a cookie?"

"You can have two cookies." Auntie Mary took Kelsey's arm and led her into the building.

Crossing her arms, Dana bit her lip. "That was scary."

"You shouldn't have focused attention on Kelsey's condition by shouting her name like that. It's bad enough Ben brought up the Redbird gift with half of Silverhill in the room."

"I had to get her out of that trance. Are you blaming me for putting Kelsey in danger?" A rush of heat claimed her chest, suffocating her.

"I'm not blaming you, Dana…for anything." He skimmed his fingers down her cheek, his cool touch almost sizzling against her warm skin. "We need to talk."

Rafe's eyes, no longer as hard as blue glass, sent a thrill of hope to her core, weakening her knees. Did he forgive her?

He cupped her face with his large hand. "Do you think you can stay here while I take Kelsey back to Auntie Mary's house? We need to find out who has that seventh ring and where Ben got the other rings. Do you feel up to that task?"

She briefly rested her cheek against his palm before straightening her spine. "I'm an FBI agent, Sheriff McClintock. I know my job. Besides, I think Kelsey is better off in your company right now. The three Redbird females do not need to be feeding off of each other's vibes."

"Did you see what Kelsey saw? I didn't want to ask her, didn't want to probe into what upset her."

"Good. Because I did get a glimpse of her vision and it wasn't pretty."

"Nothing useful?" Rafe sliced his hands through the air. "Not that I want to go there with her."

"I know that." She trailed her fingers along his forearm, tracing the corded muscle beneath his crisp white cotton shirt. She couldn't be leaving Kelsey in better hands. "Kelsey's disjointed visions had no meaning."

"The tribal rings prompted Kelsey's vision, didn't they?" Rafe's gaze strayed over Dana's head to the crowded room.

"I think so."

"Then we need to know who had possession and when."

Auntie Mary and Kelsey returned just as the party began to move to the patio for the performance of the Bear Dance. Rafe made sure his brother had a ride home and then left with Kelsey, clutching a pink-frosted cookie in her hand.

Dana didn't take a deep breath until Rafe bundled Kelsey into his truck and pulled away from the cultural center. Then she wandered back inside and hung around the edges of the crowd watching the Bear Dance.

She didn't want to alarm Kelsey…or Rafe, but the atmosphere of the cultural center had been affecting her all night. Evil hovered in the corners of the high-ceilinged, expansive room, evil she hadn't felt before on her visits here. It must be the rings.

Or maybe she needed a pink-frosted cookie too.

She broke away from the performance on the patio and sauntered to the dessert table. As Dana selected a cookie from the tray, a waiter refilled her wineglass. Great—red wine and a cookie. That should make her feel a whole lot better.

Turning, she took a bite of her cookie and her gaze locked on the display case containing the tribal rings. The drums from the performance outside reverberated in her chest. Her dry throat made it almost impossible for her to swallow the cookie, so she took a gulp of wine. And another.

The wine propped up her sagging confidence and she strolled to the display and peered inside. The majestic rings gleamed from the backlighting in the case. Dana gripped the smooth wooden edges of the case as her gaze darted from one ring to the next.

Did the malevolence emanating from the rings come from the intentions of the one who bestowed them on the tribe or from their more recent use by a serial killer?

A hand grabbed her arm and she gasped and spun around.

Joshua's handsome face split into a grin. "Whoa. I called your name three times. Were you in communication with the tribal rings or something?"

Dana licked her lips. "Don't be ridiculous. The gift passed me by, remember?"

"I remember you said that an hour ago." Joshua's smile remained in place but his eyes narrowed. "But that's not what I remember from when we were kids. You told me then you had the gift and hated it."

"That's right." Dana crumbled her cookie in a napkin and glanced at the crowd breaking up as the dance ended. "I hated the gift so much, I blocked it. I'm a totally useless shaman today." She tapped the glass. "Why won't you give your ring to Ben?"

"Didn't you hear? I don't have the ring anymore. Your stepfather cheated me out of it, and then your boyfriend confiscated it. By the way, I was surprised to hear you two have a child. You never gave it up for me."

Dana tossed her wine in Joshua's face. "When did you become such a pig?"

Ben stepped between them and handed Joshua a napkin. "Is there a problem?"

"No problem." Joshua formed a gun with his fingers and shot at Ben. "And when I get my tribal ring back from the sheriff, maybe I'll give you first dibs…for a price."

Joshua ambled away and Dana shook her head. "What is his problem?"

"He's greedy. I knew his family had one of the tribal rings, but when I approached him about loaning it to the cultural center he demanded money. None of the other owners of the rings asked for money."

"You have no idea who has the seventh ring?" Dana gripped the stem of her wineglass.

"Sadly, no."

"What about the other rings?"

Ben cocked his head. "What do you mean?"

"Who had those and when did they arrive at the cultural center?"

A few other guests clustered around the display case to view the rings as Ben reeled off several familiar Ute family names who donated the rings. "But the rings didn't arrive at the cultural center until this morning."

"What?" Dana jerked up her head.

"All of the rings, except the two not in my possession, have been safely stored at the Durango Museum of Cultural Arts."

Biting her lip, Dana hunched over the display case to study each ring. She hadn't felt anything at all from the ring Rafe took from Lenny and Joshua, but the minute she'd stepped through the doors of the cultural center tonight her senses had been on high alert. Maybe the entire atmosphere had ramped up her susceptibility to the gift. But what about Kelsey?

Dana sighed and stuffed the rest of her crumbled cookie into her mouth. She didn't know how her superpowers worked. She'd never been interested…until now.

Flawed superpowers aside, she planned to pay a visit to the Durango Museum of Cultural Arts. At this point, she trusted Ben Whitecotton about as much as she trusted her childhood friend and her stepfather.

WHEN RAFE GOT KELSEY BACK to Auntie Mary's house, Kelsey pleaded with him to let her wait up for her mother and aunt. He didn't figure she'd last that long since the long eye-lashes she'd inherited from her mom were already drooping over her eyes.

She wheedled some microwave popcorn out of him and snuggled next to him on the sofa, subjecting him to her favorite dance competition show on TV. After several minutes, he couldn't take it any more and started poking fun at the dancers and trying a few moves himself, which made her dissolve into fits of giggles.

Once they'd demolished the popcorn, he sent her to brush her teeth while he picked up their mess. Frowning, he glanced at the clock on the wall. Dana had better come back bearing news about the whereabouts of those rings, or the FBI would be moving in and taking over his investigation. He and Emmett needed a big break—any break.

Glass shattered, and Rafe dropped the kitchen towel and stumbled toward the bathroom, the blood roaring in his ears.

Kelsey was standing at the sink, clutching the edge of the vanity. The white face in the mirror had him gulping air and rushing to her side. "Kelsey! What's wrong?"

"No, no, no." She squeezed her eyes shut and shook her head from side to side.

Was she going into a trance? Dana didn't want Kelsey to have any visions, and he didn't plan on failing his first time alone with his daughter.

He grabbed her shoulders, shaking her gently while repeating her name. Dana had used ice at the cultural center. Should he splash her face with cold water? As Kelsey continued to moan, Rafe yanked on the faucet, wet his hands and patted her cheeks and brow.

Her eyelids flew open and she met Rafe's gaze in the mirror. Her dark eyes cleared and she spun around and grabbed his shirt.

"We have to save Mom."

Chapter Fifteen

Dana wandered out to the empty patio, dark since Ben ordered the fire in the pit extinguished. She'd have to get Auntie Mary home soon, but her aunt was enjoying the limelight as guests continued to pepper her with questions about the Ute culture and traditions.

She couldn't understand why the five tribal rings on display had affected both her and Kelsey, while the ring belonging to Joshua had left her cold. Maybe the killer had possession of the missing seventh ring...and had it with him tonight.

Rubbing her arms against the sudden chill, she extended her arms toward the burning embers still glowing in the fire pit. She raised her head at the loud voices coming from inside the center. She thought both Lenny and Joshua had left. She hoped they weren't going at it again.

The doors to the patio burst open, and Rafe stormed outside shouting her name. Swiveling her head around, she caught a quick movement out of the corner of her eye. Before she could focus on it, Rafe wrapped his arms around her body and tackled her to the ground.

As she fell, a whining noise passed close by her ear and

something landed with a thunk against one of the wooden benches. Rafe's body crushed hers as they toppled to the ground.

Her nose pressed into his neck and she smelled popcorn along with his usual clean, fresh scent. Had the man lost his mind?

Shocked voices and a few screams echoed around the patio, and she struggled to sit up.

One voice rose above the rest. "Good God. Where did that come from?"

Rafe finally edged off her body and pulled her against his chest. She looked over his shoulder at the horrified faces crowded at the door. She tracked the path of their gazes and cried out, digging her fingernails into Rafe's back.

A long arrow, still quivering, was embedded into the back of a wooden bench. That's what had whizzed by her head when Rafe tackled her.

She gulped in breaths of air. "Where's Kelsey?"

"She's safe at Auntie Mary's neighbor's house." He kissed her throbbing temple.

"Someone must've stolen that from the supply room." Ben strode across the patio and reached out to the arrow.

"Wait." Rafe rose, his arm still supporting Dana. "Don't touch it. There might be fingerprints."

Ben tossed his ponytail. "You expect to find fingerprints on file from some teenager?"

"Teenager? Do you think this was a practical joke?"

Dana's knees almost gave out, and she sagged against Rafe. If he hadn't removed her from the path of that arrow…

"W-what else? Some of the boys tonight were really inter-ested in the weapons. They probably stole one of the bows and arrows and thought they'd try it out."

"Does that look like target practice to you?" Rafe leveled a finger at the deadly arrow impaling the wood.

"You're not implying someone actually used a bow and arrow to try and take out Dana, are you?" Joshua stepped into the circle that was fast forming around the bench. "Why would someone want to kill Dana?"

Dana gritted her teeth and fixed Joshua with a stare.

"In case you've forgotten, we still have a serial killer on the loose and Dana is working the case." Rafe settled her on another bench and rubbed a spot on her cheek with the pad of his thumb.

"Yeah, but a bow and arrow isn't his M.O. and you're working the case too, along with Emmett and that other FBI guy." Joshua crossed his arms and tapped the toe of his boot. "Unless the killer thinks Dana's using her gift to discover his true identity."

"If I could do that, I would've done it a long time ago and saved a few lives. You're an idiot, Joshua." Dana ran her hands through her hair. "The more I think about it, Rafe, the more I think Ben might be right. Some of the boys kept trying to handle the weapons. Let's check it out."

Emmett had already gone home, so Rafe called him to help canvass the area. After reassuring Auntie Mary and sending her home with one of her friends, Dana followed Rafe outside.

She told him about the tribal rings and Ben's claim that the five rings had been locked up at the Durango Museum of Cultural Arts until that morning. "That means the killer didn't have access to any of those five rings, and it has to be Joshua's ring or the missing one that the killer is wearing when he strangles those women."

"Or Ben's lying."

Rafe gave voice to her own worry. Dana brushed her hair off her face and tucked it behind her ear. "That's why I plan to take a trip to Durango tomorrow."

"And I'm coming with you. I have a few questions I want to ask Joshua's employees at his clubs."

"Okay, now tell me what you're doing here?" She bunched the folds of her skirt in her hands. "How did you know I was in danger?"

"Kelsey. She had a vision or something when she was in the bathroom brushing her teeth." Rafe looked down and kicked the ground. "I never should've left her alone in there."

She laid a hand on his forearm. She'd done this to him—made him doubt himself as a father. "Believe me, she's been brushing her teeth alone for years. The important thing is you brought her out of the trance and saved my life."

"If she hadn't felt your danger…" Rafe crushed her to his chest and laid his cheek against the top of her head. "I might have lost you forever."

His heart, sure and steady, thudded against her own. "Does this mean you forgive me, Rafe? I made a terrible mistake."

He placed two fingers against her lips.

The gravel crunched behind them and they jumped apart. Emmett strode forward, shaking his head. "On top of a serial killer, we have some nut running around with bows and arrows? Have you canvassed the area yet, discovered the bow?"

Reluctantly, Dana left the safety of Rafe's embrace and for the next hour she, Rafe, Emmett and one of Emmett's officers searched the area around the cultural center and the supply room inside.

Emmett found the bow used to launch the arrow shoved into the branches of a bush, but they didn't find any fingerprints on the bow or the arrow, even though someone had stolen both from the supply room.

Rafe questioned the guests, but nobody noticed anyone near the supply room and there were too many people coming and going for anyone to notice any one guest's absence.

As the last of the detained guests left and the catering staff cleaned up after the revelers, Dana, Rafe and Emmett huddled on the patio. Emmett tossed a stone into the fire pit. "The person who took a potshot at you is just as stealthy as our Headband Killer. Do you think he's one and the same? He warned you when you first got here, Dana. I guess you didn't listen."

"I think it is the same person. Listen Ben, Rafe and I are onto something involving those tribal rings. Do you remember the round, red mark on the victims' necks?"

Emmett narrowed his eyes, his gaze shifting between the two of them. "You think one of the tribal rings made that mark?"

"Maybe." Rafe placed a hand on the curve of her back as a warning.

"Did the rings scare your little girl tonight?" Emmett sawed his lower lip with his teeth.

"She had an upset stomach from too much sugar and excitement, Emmett. That's it." Rafe laced his fingers with Dana's and tugged. "Now her mom wants to make sure she's okay."

Rafe bundled Dana into her car. "I'll follow you to Auntie Mary's, and then I'll pick you up tomorrow for Durango."

Dana sensed he didn't want to let her out of his sight…and she liked it. "I'm just going across the reservation."

He kissed her on the mouth and smacked the roof of her car. "Yeah, that's what I'm afraid of."

THE FOLLOWING DAY, Rafe swung by Auntie Mary's to pick up Dana for their mission in Durango. While Dana strapped on her holster in the bedroom, she listened to Kelsey's bright chatter with Rafe.

Thank God Kelsey had recovered from her scare last night. She hadn't succumbed to another vision, but her strong sense of foreboding regarding Dana had frightened her.

"My mom is flying back with me to Denver tomorrow morning." Kelsey glanced up at him through lowered lashes. "Will you come visit me?"

"Absolutely. I have to watch that dance show with you to find out who wins."

"Then what?" She jerked her thumb toward Dana. "What's going to happen with you and Mom?"

"That's for us to figure out." Dana playfully yanked Kelsey's ponytail.

Rafe placed a hand on Kelsey's head. "Whatever happens, I'm your father, and I'm going to take that very seriously. Is that okay with you?"

Kelsey nodded, grinning ear to ear.

When they got into Rafe's squad car, Dana turned to him. "She adores you already. Thanks for reassuring her. She needed to hear that even though we might not be together, you'll be there for her."

"About that…"

Dana's breath hitched in her throat, and she dug through her purse for some lip gloss to hide her expression of hope. He'd mentioned something about not blaming her right before he took Kelsey home and all hell broke loose. She'd been holding those words close to her heart, afraid of bringing them into the light and examining them too closely.

As the silence stretched, she stole a glance at his strong hands, gripping the steering wheel as if ready for takeoff. Then he blew out a breath.

"I found out that Pam knew about your pregnancy and that she used intimidation and threats to keep it from me and drive you out of town."

She dropped her purse, its contents spilling onto the floor of the car. Had Pam confessed everything to put her own spin on it? From the tone of Rafe's voice, Pam hadn't put a very successful spin on her side of the story.

"D-did Pam tell you what happened?"

"Yeah, but not out of the goodness of her heart." His lips twisted into a bitter smile. "My brother forced her into it."

Rafe then launched into Rod's discovery of a McClintock half brother and how he'd overheard Pam talking to Ralph about Dana's pregnancy and the means she had used to convince Dana to keep the baby a secret.

"You have another brother out there somewhere?"

Rafe jerked the steering wheel. "That's not the point. When I found out about Kelsey, why didn't you tell me Pam knew everything and threatened you?"

She shrugged. "What was the point of that? I went along with it. I deceived you, and I continued to deceive you even after Pam no longer held any sway over me."

"You took all the blame onto yourself."

"I deserved the blame."

The buzz of her cell phone saved Dana from hearing whether or not Rafe agreed with her, but the voice on the other end of the line did nothing to calm her nerves.

"Dana, it's Steve. Meetings are over, and I'm flying back tomorrow."

"Sounds like bad news."

Rafe clutched her arm. "Kelsey?"

She shook her head. Rafe was getting a crash course in the perils and pitfalls of parenthood. "Steve, I'm in the car with Sheriff McClintock. Can I put you on speaker?"

He agreed and she switched her cell to speaker.

"Hey, Sheriff. The Bureau is not happy with the investigation. It's not a reflection on you or your department or Emmett. The fact that Dr. Simpson withheld information from an autopsy didn't help, although my bosses were impressed you got that out of him. We had that serial killer on an Indian reservation several years ago and we never caught the guy. The FBI took a black eye on that one, with Native American groups accusing us of insensitivity and taking a cavalier attitude because the victims were Native Americans. We're not too anxious to go down that road again."

Dana clenched her teeth. She didn't want to give up this investigation—not when they were so close. "That was years ago, Steve. We're on our way right now…"

Rafe squeezed her thigh and put his finger to his lips. "I get it, Steve. When's the new task force coming down?"

"In about a week, Rafe. Look, I know it's tough when the Bureau moves in on local law enforcement, but this is a delicate situation. Of course, we're going to set up meetings with you and Emmett to review the cases."

They spent the rest of the drive into Durango on the phone with Steve. Dana marveled at Rafe's restraint. She figured he'd be hitting the roof of the car about now. But at least Steve's call gave her a reprieve in discussing their own delicate situation.

They ended the call as they pulled into the parking lot of one of Joshua's clubs, Bare Elegance. Dana slipped her cell back into her purse. "Why didn't you want to tell Steve about our lead?"

"Let's see how it pans out first. We have no solid evidence the killer wore a ring when he strangled those women, and even less evidence that the ring was one of the seven Ute tribal rings. All we have is you, and if that flying arrow last night means the Headband Killer has figured out you're using the gift to track him down, we need to stop him now or get you out of Silverhill."

"I'm not leaving. I'll be staying on with the task force, so get used to it."

"We'll see about that."

They dropped the subject when they entered Joshua's opulent club, all mirrors, red velvet and black leather, bu questioning Joshua's employees got them nowhere. He eithe elicited fierce loyalty or they knew nothing about his ring.

After their fruitless questioning, they drove across town to the Durango Museum of Cultural Arts, hoping to get a line on the missing seventh ring.

Dana approached the information counter while Rafe studied a rock painting.

"I'd like to see the curator, Adam Reynolds." She flipped out her FBI badge.

The woman at the desk picked up the phone and two minutes later, a tall, spindly man with long silver hair wearing hiking sandals and socks scuffed across the polished floor.

"Can I help you…?"

"Agent Dana Croft." Dana thrust out her hand. "And this is Sheriff McClintock from Silverhill."

They shook hands and Mr. Reynolds led them back to his messy office, crammed with books, magazines and boxes Dana exchanged a look with Rafe. Was he thinking what she was thinking? Had he stored the rings in there with all this other junk?

Dana scooped up a stack of file folders from a chair and dropped them on Mr. Reynolds's desk before settling in the chair. Rafe stood, wedging a shoulder against the doorjamb.

"I'm going to get right to the point, Mr. Reynolds." Dana folded her hands in her lap and leaned forward. "We're looking for the seventh Ute tribal ring. We know Ben Whitecotton curator of the Southern Ute Cultural Center, now has five of the rings in his possession, and we know the location of a sixth ring, but nobody seems to know where the seventh ring is."

Mr. Reynolds spread his hands. "I can't help you. I've searched for it before, but nobody has stepped forward. I helped Ben round up a couple of those rings, but we never could locate the seventh."

"That's the second reason why we're here. We'd like the information about who had these rings. Can you provide us with that?"

Reynolds spun in his chair to face a four-drawer filing cabinet. "I know it may not look like it to you, but I have a rather precise filing system here."

Rafe rolled his eyes at Dana while Reynolds pawed through one of the filing cabinet drawers. He withdrew a thick manila folder. "I'm afraid I'll have to make a copy of everything in the folder before handing it over to you. That could take a few hours, and my assistant doesn't work on Sundays. Can I get it to you tomorrow?"

Biting her lip, Dana glanced at Rafe. She'd be on an airplane tomorrow taking Kelsey home.

"I can come back tomorrow to pick it up." Rafe shoved off the wall and shook hands with Reynolds. "Thanks for your help."

"I'm sorry I have to make you wait because I gather this is a matter of some urgency. However, I'm rather particular about security issues, believe it or not."

"I'm sure that's why Ben entrusted the tribal rings to your care until he opened the cultural center." Dana replaced the file folders on the chair. Wouldn't want to disrupt his precise filing methods.

"Excuse me?" The curator raised his brows as he pushed back from his chair.

"The five tribal rings. Ben told me he put them in your care for safekeeping until the opening of the Southern Ute Cultural Center."

Reynolds shook his head. "You must've misunderstood, Agent Croft. I helped Ben locate those tribal rings over a year ago, but I never had possession of them. As we found each one, Ben kept them locked in a safe or something. I never actually inquired. He had a lot of priceless artifacts under his care. The rings comprised just another asset to be secured."

Rafe slammed the office door he'd just opened and the beveled pane of glass in the door trembled. "Are you telling us Ben Whitecotton had those five rings for over a year?"

Reynolds's gaze darted between Rafe and Dana as his white skin grew paler. "N-not all of them. It took us several months to locate all five of the rings."

"But he had at least one of the rings for the past three months?" Hunching forward, Rafe gripped the back of the chair.

"In the past three months? All but one, I believe."

They thanked him for his time and information and practically ran out of his office. When they burst outside the museum, they both spun toward each other.

Rafe cursed. "Ben had those rings all along."

"And even more damning is that he lied to me about it." Dana hugged herself in the chill that was spreading with the rapidly sinking sun.

"We need to make a return visit to the cultural center and ask him why." Rafe dug in his front pocket for his keys.

"I can't believe it. Why would Ben want to kill those women? He's all about preserving our Ute culture, why would he murder Ute women?"

"Think about those women, Dana." Rafe cranked on the engine. "They weren't pure. In some way, they sullied the proud Ute culture. Even Alicia wound up pregnant and unwed. Ben must've hated that."

"Ben must've gone off the deep end. I wonder if it started when his wife left him."

"I don't care when it started or how. We need to stop him. Who knows how many impure Ute women he's eyeing right now?"

Dana dug her nails into her palms as Rafe sped down the highway. "Maybe it's not Ben. Maybe somebody took a ring from him. That seventh ring is still missing."

"Then why did he lie to you about the whereabouts of those rings? He had them all along, at the time of all the murders. Did he know you were coming here today?"

"I—I don't think I mentioned it."

As they cruised to the edge of Silverhill, Dana's cell phone buzzed and she frowned at the unknown number on the display before flipping open the phone. "Hello?"

"Dana, it's Auntie Mary. I'm at Margie's house. She's having a terrible time with her arthritis."

"Is Kelsey with you?"

"No, that's why I'm calling. I left her next door with the Johnsons."

The tightness in Dana's chest eased. "We have a stop to make, but if I get back before you do let the Johnsons know I'll pick up Kelsey."

"That's just it, Dana. Kelsey's not with the Johnsons anymore."

"Where is she?" Dana placed a hand across her stomach to calm the sudden flight of butterflies.

"She's with Ben at the cultural center."

DANA ALMOST DOUBLED OVER in the seat next to him. Rafe's hand shot out to sweep the hair from her face. "What's wrong?"

She clamped the phone against her thigh and choked on a sob. "Ben has Kelsey."

The blood pounded in his ears and his foot jammed on the accelerator. Ben knew about Kelsey's gift. He'd witnessed it last night and knew what it meant.

Dana managed to calm her voice and finish the conversation with Auntie Mary, and then she dropped the phone on the floor of the car. "Auntie Mary left her with the Johnsons while she visited a friend, and Ben came to the Johnsons to ask if Kelsey wanted to go to the cultural center with him."

"And they just let her go?"

"They've known Ben for years. We all have." She buried her face in her hands. "He knows, doesn't he? He knows about both me and Kelsey. He tried to kill me last night with that arrow, and he must have figured I'd check out his story at the Durango museum. What's he going to do to Kelsey?"

"He's not going to lay a finger on her, not while I have one breath left in my body." He stroked Dana's heaving shoulder. "Don't worry. We'll get her back. We need to act like law enforcement here, not parents."

Dana wiped her face and blew her nose. "Should we call Emmett or Brice?"

"At this point, I'm sure we can get there before they can. Besides, what are we going to tell them? So far we have no evidence that Ben has done anything wrong."

"He took Kelsey."

"With your aunt's permission."

"Do you think he really brought her to the cultural center?"

"I don't know, but that's the first place we're going to check."

Rafe swung his car into the darkened parking lot of the cultural center. Without the lights and crowd, the setting felt eerie. Yeah, now that he knew the curator was a killer...and had his daughter.

As they crept up the front steps, Dana pulled out her

weapon. Blinds covered the windows in the front, but a soft, flickering glow emanated between the slats.

Rafe tried the front door, which was locked, and whispered, "Can you see where that light's coming from? Is it the back office?"

Dana jumped from the veranda and crouched next to a side window. She twisted her head to the side, her brows knitted. "It's coming from the patio, and it looks like the light is from a fire."

"We can get to the patio from the back of the building." Rafe pulled Dana behind him. "Follow me."

They slid along the side of the building until they got to the stucco wall that surrounded the outdoor patio. Low murmuring wafted over the wall, and Dana grabbed Rafe's back pocket.

"That's Ben's voice."

He took her hand and led her around the corner. He remembered a gate in the back, probably how Ben slipped out of the party last night to get into position to shoot that arrow at Dana.

The black wrought-iron gate stood open to the wild underbrush that encircled the cultural center. Tucking Dana behind him, Rafe approached the gate and peered into the patio.

His hand tightened on his gun as a blazing fury engulfed his body. Ben was seated on one side of the fire pit, pointing a gun at Kelsey, seated across from him, her eyes wide.

Ben raised his voice, "Come in, Rafe. I've been expecting you. Dana too."

Dana cried out as she stumbled around Rafe and onto the patio. "What are you doing? Let her go."

Ben smiled. "I can't do that. Do you know, Dana, our particular Ute tribe is the only one where the gift is concentrated in females only. I've been doing a lot of research in setting up this cultural center, and I've discovered that some of the other Ute tribes forcibly wrenched this power from the females. Now I have the perfect opportunity to try it out. I've been dabbling, you know, but the wolf spirit didn't like it."

"Ben, why did you kill those women?" Dana took a step toward Kelsey.

Ben raised his weapon. "Both of you need to drop your guns and shove them over here. If you don't, I'll shoot your daughter and will just have to give up on my scheme of transferring her power to me. But then you won't have a daughter anymore."

Dana dropped her gun immediately and kicked it toward the fire circle.

Rafe clenched his jaw. He didn't even have his backup weapon with him, but he couldn't risk Kelsey's life. He tossed his gun under one of the benches.

"Very wise decision." Ben waved his gun at Dana. "Join your daughter. Now I'll be able to pull the power from both of you. In your case, two is better than one because it's most likely weak since it's so diluted. You're only half Ute, Dana, and you tainted your daughter's blood even more by saddling her with a white man as a father."

Dana settled next to Kelsey and gathered her in a hug. "It's okay, sweetie."

Kelsey buried her head against Dana's shoulder. "I'm sorry, Mom. I knew I shouldn't have come with him because I had bad feelings about him and this place, but I thought maybe I could help you."

"It's not your fault." She stroked Kelsey's ponytail. "If we transfer our gift to you, Ben, will you let us go?"

Ben snorted. "You know I committed those murders. I can't let any of you go. As soon as you started showing interest in those rings, I knew my mission was over. I never feared

Emmett or the FBI would catch me, but when you showed up, I figured you were here to use your powers to find me. Nobody had linked the rings to the murders until your daughter reacted last night when I brought them out. Then you started asking questions about them. I knew it was only a matter of time before you discovered I had the rings in my possession at the time of the murders."

Rafe exchanged a glance with Dana. "Did you kill those young women because they didn't meet your standards of a proper Ute? Did you fancy yourself one of those old chiefs, keeping everyone in line? You should do a little more research, Ben. They didn't murder members of their own tribe."

"Shut up, Rafe. I don't need an outsider to tell me my cultural history. Sit on that bench behind Dana and your daughter where I can see you while I perform my ritual."

Rafe lowered himself to the bench, his knees almost touching Dana's back. If he had the chance, he'd lunge forward and take the bullet for her or his daughter.

He didn't even know of Kelsey's existence three days ago, and now he was willing to die for her.

Dana cleared her throat. "Did you attack me outside of Auntie Mary's house when I first arrived?"

Ben nodded. "I used the power I had learned from my research to immobilize you, but I encountered the wolf. Not that I planned to harm you…then."

"And what about the rock? Did you use your newfound powers to sneak onto the McClintock ranch and throw that rock through Rafe's window?"

"Joshua did that in a fit of jealousy." Ben tilted his head. "You haven't asked about the bow and arrow."

Rafe shifted on the bench. Ben sounded offended she

hadn't asked. They were definitely dealing with someone unhinged…which might make taking him down easier.

"Do I need to ask? You noticed my interest in the rings and decided to get rid of me."

To stall for more time, Rafe asked him about Brice's cell phone.

Ben snorted. "Your deputy was too busy with Belinda Mathers to notice I slipped his phone from his jacket. I knew I could lure Jacey to the Shopco parking lot with a text message from Brice."

Ben laced his fingers and cracked his knuckles. "That's really quite enough. I tried to rid the tribe of women unworthy of their Ute heritage. I used the headband to signify their status as fake Native Americans, and then dumped their bodies in the construction sites scarring our land. But that's over now. Before you and your daughter pass on to the next world, I'm going to take your power as my own and become a Ute shaman."

Ben had several jars next to him, and with his free hand he began to pinch the contents of the jars between his fingers and toss the substances into the fire. He started to chant, and Kelsey's chin dropped to her chest.

Dana moaned and her spine stiffened. Rafe reached for her, but Ben stopped him by leveling his gun at her.

"Hold it there, Rafe."

Would Ben go into a trance as a result of this mumbo jumbo too? All Rafe's senses went on high alert, waiting for an opportunity to strike.

Kelsey slumped against her mother. Dana jerked up her head, pulling back her shoulders while chanting in a low voice. Startled, Ben dropped one of the jars, which cracked against the patio tile.

Dana's voice rose, drowning out Ben's. Rafe didn't know if Dana was pretending or not, but her incantations were affecting Ben. His hands shook as he sprinkled some orange powder into the fire, creating a burst of flame.

Rafe tensed his muscles, wedging his palms against the seat of the bench, rising on the balls of his feet.

Ben yelled, "Stop! Stop trying to block me." His gun wavered as he pointed it at Dana.

Ben's eyes bulged from their sockets as a scream ripped from his throat, "The wolf!"

Staggering to his feet, Ben clutched his weapon with a shaking hand. Rafe lunged from the bench and jumped across the fire. He tackled Ben as Ben squeezed off a shot. Rafe clinched Ben's wrist in a vise and forced the gun from his hand. With his other hand, Ben grabbed the can of lighter fluid and chucked it into the fire.

The flames roared to life, searing Rafe's back. Leaving Ben writhing on the ground, Rafe skirted the fire, which licked at the wooden benches around the pit, and scooped up Kelsey in his arms. He pushed Dana back from the fire circle and hooked an arm around her waist, dragging her backward toward the open gate.

An explosion rocked the ground, propelling them forward and into the bushes. Rafe covered Dana and Kelsey with his body, and then scrambled to his feet, clutching Kelsey against his chest. Pulling Dana up against him, he asked, "Can you walk?"

"I'm fine. Is Kelsey okay?"

He glanced down into his daughter's face, her lashes stirring against her cheeks. "She's gonna be."

Grasping Dana's arm, he pulled her around the corner of

the wall into the parking lot. The fire from the patio had spread to the cultural center building, engulfing one side.

They stood side by side watching the flames leap into the night sky.

Dana squeezed Rafe's hand. "He's in there, isn't he?"

Rafe nodded. "It's where he belongs."

Epilogue

"He confessed to both of us and then took his own life by jumping into the fire." Rafe dropped a stack of file folders in front of Agent Steve Lubeck. "Just trying to weed out the riffraff from the Southern Ute tribe."

"You two did a great job." Steve shoved the folders into his briefcase. "How did you figure out that mark on the girls' throats came from one of those tribal rings?"

Dana held her breath while Rafe lifted a shoulder. "Call it a hunch."

Steve rapped his knuckles on the stack of folders. "I'll call it a gift and leave it at that."

As Steve got to the door of the Silverhill sheriff's station, he grabbed the handle and turned. "Enjoy your time off, Dana. We'll put you back to work when you return."

Dana blew out a breath as the door slammed shut. "I hope Steve doesn't expect me to use my gift for every murder case we get."

"About that. You never did tell me whether or not your chanting brought the wolf spirit. I sure as heck didn't see or hear any wolf on that patio."

"Maybe it did. Ben saw the wolf, so perhaps my chant

came from somewhere deep inside." She shrugged. "I really didn't have the slightest idea what I was saying."

An hour later, Dana hopped out of Rafe's truck to unlatch the gate leading to the McClintock ranch. Ralph and Pam had insisted on throwing a party for their newly discovered grand-daughter before Dana took her back to Denver. Whether or not they'd stay in Denver she didn't know. She and Rafe never did finish that conversation.

Rafe pulled to a stop in front of the house and turned to Kelsey in the backseat. "Are you ready? You have a couple of uncles in there, an aunt, a cousin and some grandparents."

"Let's do this." Kelsey clenched her hand for a fist bump, and Rafe's knuckles met hers.

Dana rolled her eyes before they could tear up. "You two are the most social animals I know. Kelsey's going to have the McClintock clan wrapped around her little finger in no time."

As Rafe winked at his daughter and she grinned back, one of those tears trembled on the edge of Dana's eyelashes. Then the McClintocks surged onto the front porch and engulfed her and Kelsey in a sea of love and acceptance. Even Pam showed a face of contrition and invited Kelsey and her little cousin, Shelby, to help her in the kitchen.

After they ate, Julia, the wife of Rafe's middle brother, Ryder, took the girls to the barn to see the horses and baby foal born two days before. The McClintock men settled in the family room, and Pam brought bottles of beer to her stepsons and poured a shot of whiskey for her husband.

Ralph threw back the shot in one gulp and planted his gnarled hands on his knees. "I suppose you're all anxious to hear about your half brother. Rod knows a little, probably more than he wants to know."

These McClintocks led complicated lives. Dana perched on the arm of the sofa next to Rafe, and he curled an arm around her waist while Ralph told his sons about their half brother and his mother.

"So, you see, I offered the little gal money to take care of the baby, but she didn't want anything from me. Skipped town before she even had the child."

Rod jumped up from his chair and paced to the window. "You mean you tried to pay her off so she'd leave town and take the baby with her."

A pain sliced through Dana's temple. That story hit too close to home. Rafe squeezed her hip.

Ryder asked, "Where is this brother now?"

"Works in private security." Ralph hunched his shoulders. "Moves around a lot."

Dana patted Rafe's thigh. "I'm going to watch the girls."

He rose with her and followed her outside to the paddock to watch Kelsey, Shelby and Julia with one of the ranch hands and the baby foal.

Dana hung over the fence and waved. "She looks right at home."

"She is."

Turning to face him, Dana leaned against the fence. "I did a foolish thing keeping her from you, Rafe."

His rough palm skimmed her cheek. "I know you did."

"And honestly? I didn't just do it for you because I thought your father would disown you. I did it to protect myself and my pride."

"I know that too, sweetheart, but at eighteen we don't have much more than our pride."

"But I had so much more, Rafe. I had you, and I had our child. That should've been enough."

"Is it enough now?" He placed both hands on her shoulders and drew her toward his warmth.

She gazed into his eyes and they never looked bluer. She couldn't resist him any more than she could years ago. "It's enough for me. Is it enough for you?"

His answer came in the form of a hard, possessive kiss. Then he weaved a hand through her hair, pulling her closer still, and that possessive kiss changed into something sweeter…something lasting.

Rafe finally broke away, leaving her breathless but wanting more. He held up one finger and then wound it around a lock of her hair. "Just a warning—I'm nothing like my father, you're nothing like your mother and this is forever. I'll never let you go."

To prove his point, he captured her lips in fiery kiss that weakened her knees. She sighed as she snuggled against him.

She belonged in Silverhill. He was the Sheriff of Silverhill. And she'd never leave him again.

* * * * *

Up next, sparks fly when hard-nosed Rod McClintock
meets his match in a feisty runaway bride!
Look for it this spring
from Carol Ericson and only in
Harlequin Intrigue!

*Fan favorite Leslie Kelly is bringing her
readers a fantasy so scandalous,
we're calling it FORBIDDEN!*

*Look for
PLAY WITH ME
Available February 2010
from Harlequin® Blaze™.*

"AREN'T YOU GOING TO SAY 'Fly me' or at least 'Welcome Aboard'?"

Amanda Bauer didn't. The softly muttered word that actually came out of her mouth was a lot less welcoming. And had fewer letters. Four, to be exact.

The man shook his head and tsked. "Not exactly the friendly skies. Haven't caught the spirit yet this morning?"

"Make one more airline-slogan crack and you'll be walking to Chicago," she said.

He nodded once, then pushed his sunglasses onto the top of his tousled hair. The move revealed blue eyes that matched the sky above. And yeah. They were twinkling. Damn it.

"Understood. Just, uh, promise me you'll say 'Coffee, tea or me' at least once, okay? Please?"

Amanda tried to glare, but that twinkle sucked the annoyance right out of her. She could only draw in a slow breath as he climbed into the plane. As she watched her passenger disappear into the small jet, she had to wonder about the trip she was about to take.

Coffee and tea they had, and he was welcome to them. But her? Well, she'd never even considered making a move on a customer before. Talk about unprofessional.

And yet…

Something inside her suddenly wanted to take a chance, to be a little outrageous.

How long since she had done indecent things—or decent ones, for that matter—with a sexy man? Not since before they'd thrown all their energies into expanding Clear-Blue Air, at the very least. She hadn't had time for a lunch date, much less the kind of lust-fest she'd enjoyed in her younger years. The kind that lasted for entire weekends and involved not leaving a bed except to grab the kind of sensuous food that could be smeared onto—and eaten off—someone else's hot, naked, sweat-tinged body.

She closed her eyes, her hand clenching tight on the railing. Her heart fluttered in her chest and she tried to make herself move. But she couldn't—not climbing up, but not backing away, either. Not physically, and not in her head.

Was she really considering this? God, she hadn't even looked at the stranger's left hand to make sure he was available. She had no idea if he was actually attracted to her or just an irrepressible flirt. Yet something inside was telling her to take a shot with this man.

It was crazy. Something she'd never considered. Yet right now, at this moment, she was definitely considering it. If he was available…could she do it? Seduce a stranger. Have an anonymous fling, like something out of a blue movie on late-night cable?

She didn't know. All she knew was that the flight to Chicago was a short one so she had to decide quickly. And as she put her foot on the bottom step and began to climb up, Amanda suddenly had to wonder if she was about to embark on the ride of her life.

Do you have a forbidden fantasy?

Amanda Bauer does. She's always craved a life
of adventure…sexual adventure, that is. And
when she meets Reese Campbell, she knows he's
just the man to play with. And play they do. Every
few months they get together for days of wild sex,
no strings attached—or so they think….

Sneak away with:

Play with Me

by LESLIE KELLY

*Available February 2010
wherever Harlequin books are sold.*

red-hot reads

HARLEQUIN® *Blaze*™

It all started
with a few naughty books....

As a member of the Red Tote Book Club,
Carol Snow has been studying works of
classic erotic literature…but Carol doesn't
believe in love…or marriage. It's going to take
another kind of classic—Charles Dickens's
A Christmas Carol—and a little otherworldly
persuasion to convince her to go after her
own sexily ever after.

Cuddle up with

Her Sexy Valentine
by STEPHANIE BOND

Available February 2010

---

red-hot reads

HARLEQUIN
Ambassadors

Want to share your passion for reading Harlequin® Books?

Become a Harlequin Ambassador!

Harlequin Ambassadors are a group of passionate and well-connected readers who are willing to share their joy of reading Harlequin® books with family and friends.

You'll be sent all the tools you need to spark great conversation, including free books!

All we ask is that you share the romance with your friends and family!

You'll also be invited to have a say in new book ideas and exchange opinions with women just like you!

To see if you qualify* to be a Harlequin Ambassador, please visit www.HarlequinAmbassadors.com.

*Please note that not everyone who applies to be a Harlequin Ambassador will qualify. For more information please visit www.HarlequinAmbassadors.com.

Thank you for your participation.

BAP09BPA

Sold, bought, bargained for or bartered

He'll take his…

Bride on Approval

Whether there's a debt to be paid,
a will to be obeyed or a business
to be saved…she has no choice
but to say, "I do"!

PURE PRINCESS,
BARTERED BRIDE
by *Caitlin Crews*
#2894

Available February 2010!

REQUEST YOUR FREE BOOKS!

2 FREE NOVELS
PLUS 2
FREE GIFTS!

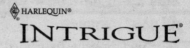

♦ HARLEQUIN®

INTRIGUE®

Breathtaking Romantic Suspense

YES! Please send me 2 FREE Harlequin Intrigue® novels and my 2 FREE gifts (gifts are worth about $10). After receiving them, if I don't wish to receive any more books, I can return the shipping statement marked "cancel." If I don't cancel, I will receive 6 brand-new novels every month and be billed just $4.24 per book in the U.S. or $4.99 per book in Canada. That's a saving of close to 15% off the cover price! It's quite a bargain! Shipping and handling is just 50¢ per book in the U.S. and 75¢ per book in Canada.* I understand that accepting the 2 free books and gifts places me under no obligation to buy anything. I can always return a shipment and cancel at any time. Even if I never buy another book from Harlequin, the two free books and gifts are mine to keep forever.

182 HDN E4EC   382 HDN E4EN

Name	(PLEASE PRINT)	
Address		Apt. #
City	State/Prov.	Zip/Postal Code

Signature (if under 18, a parent or guardian must sign)

Mail to the **Harlequin Reader Service**:
IN U.S.A.: P.O. Box 1867, Buffalo, NY 14240-1867
IN CANADA: P.O. Box 609, Fort Erie, Ontario L2A 5X3

Not valid for current subscribers to Harlequin Intrigue books.

**Are you a subscriber to Harlequin Intrigue books and
want to receive the larger-print edition? Call 1-800-873-8635 today!**

* Terms and prices subject to change without notice. Prices do not include applicable taxes. N.Y. residents add applicable sales tax. Canadian residents will be charged applicable provincial taxes and GST. Offer not valid in Quebec. This offer is limited to one order per household. All orders subject to approval. Credit or debit balances in a customer's account(s) may be offset by any other outstanding balance owed by or to the customer. Please allow 4 to 6 weeks for delivery. Offer available while quantities last.

Your Privacy: Harlequin is committed to protecting your privacy. Our Privacy Policy is available online at www.eHarlequin.com or upon request from the Reader Service. From time to time we make our lists of customers available to reputable third parties who may have a product or service of interest to you. If you would prefer we not share your name and address, please check here. ☐

Help us get it right—We strive for accurate, respectful and relevant communications. To clarify or modify your communication preferences, visit us at www.ReaderService.com/consumerschoice.

Stay up-to-date on all your romance-reading news with the brand-new Harlequin *Inside Romance*!

The Harlequin *Inside Romance* is a **FREE** quarterly newsletter highlighting our upcoming series releases and promotions!

Click on the *Inside Romance* link on the front page of www.eHarlequin.com or e-mail us at InsideRomance@Harlequin.ca to sign up to receive your FREE newsletter today!